"Did Mama finally decide to take a rest?"

"Yes. I think watching you swing from the trees and seeing me get hurt was too much for her."

Derrick looked into Elise's eyes. "Seeing you get injured was almost too much for me. How is your arm? It looks really bad."

Elise looked down and could see that the bruise on her arm was turning blue-black. "It looks worse than it feels."

"I doubt that, but I have a feeling you aren't going to tell me how bad it really hurts." He reached up and tucked an escaping tendril of hair behind her ear. "I really am sorry, Elise. Please call me if you need to lift anything heavy or if you need anything at all."

His nearness had her breath catching in her throat once more. All she could manage was a nod as she turned to the sink and began to wash pots, jars, and lids.

JANET LEE BARTON and her husband, Dan, have recently moved to Oklahoma and feel blessed to have at least one daughter and her family living nearby. Janet loves being able to share her faith and love of the Lord through her writing. She's very happy that the kind of romances the Lord has called her to write can be read by and shared with women of all ages.

Books by Janet Lee Barton

HEARTSONG PRESENTS

Stirring Up Romance

Janet Lee Barton

Heartsong Presents

To My Lord and Savior for showing me the way. And to the family He has blessed me with for your unfailing encouragement and love. I love you all.

A note from the Author:
I love to hear from my readers! You may correspond with me by writing:

Janet Lee Barton
Author Relations
PO Box 721
Uhrichsville, OH 44683

ISBN 978-1-59789-615-3

STIRRING UP ROMANCE

Our mission is to publish and distribute inspirational products offering exceptional value and biblical encouragement to the masses.

PRINTED IN THE U.S.A.

one

While Elise prepared afternoon tea, her mother-in-law, Frieda Morgan, reread the letter she'd brought in from the post office earlier that afternoon. As Elise turned to bring the tea tray to the kitchen table, her mother-in-law looked up from the pages she held.

"Elise, dear, I think it's time I take Derrick up on his invitation to come live with him."

Elise almost dropped the full tray, but she steadied herself just before she reached the table. She set the tray down as quickly as she could while her mind screamed, *No, Mama. Please don't go.*

She took a seat at the table and busied herself pouring their tea while she fought to sound calm. "Mama, are you sure this is what you want to do?"

"Elise, I do not want to leave you. But Derrick has been asking me to come live with him down in Farmington for several years. It sounds as though he could use my help with the harvest this year. He says his orchard will produce a record crop if the weather holds. I know I could help him out by cooking for those who come to help pick the apples."

"But, Mama, you haven't been feeling at all well these last few months. I'm not sure you're up to the trip, not to mention the work once you get there." Elise went through the motions of stirring cream and sugar into her tea, but her heart was breaking

5

at the thought that her husband's mother might move away. She'd come to love her as her own mother. With her husband, Carl, and both of her parents gone now, Elise's only remaining relative was Frieda Morgan.

"It will take a few weeks to get ready. I'm sure I'll feel better by the time we get all the arrangements made." Frieda paused and took a sip of tea. "You will help me with all that, won't you, dear?"

Hard as it would be to see her go, Elise loved her mother-in-law enough that she wanted her to be happy. "Of course I will, if it's what you want. But only if you promise to come visit me."

"Oh, dear Elise, you are my daughter. Of course I will. Perhaps I'll stay part of the year with Derrick and part of the year with you. But I just feel that Derrick needs me right now."

Elise felt somewhat better knowing that Frieda wasn't deserting her. She took a sip from her cup of tea. Besides, it would be selfish of her to try to talk her mother-in-law out of going to her son. She sighed. "I'll get the train schedule for you tomorrow so you can start planning your trip."

Frieda reached across the table and patted her hand. "Thank you, dear. I knew you would understand."

"I do. I just hate to see you go."

"I know. And I hate to leave you behind. You and Carl were so kind to invite me into your home after Papa died. And then for you to ask me to stay when Carl passed away. . . You're a wonderful daughter to me, Elise. I could ask for no better."

"Oh, Mama, don't be talking like that. You'll have me bawling like a newborn babe. I'll check into everything for you. But I won't let you get on a train by yourself if you aren't feeling much better than you've been the past few weeks."

"I'm going to be fine, dear. You'll see. But I'd be more than happy for you to accompany me to Farmington."

Elise was quiet for a few moments. She wouldn't have to worry about Frieda if she did go with her, and there was really no reason not to go. Carl had left her with a modest inheritance. The home she and her mother-in-law lived in was paid for, there was a tidy sum in the bank, and Elise had her sewing and cooking skills to fall back on, should she ever need to work.

"Perhaps I'll go with you to make sure you're all right once you get to Farmington. I'd feel better helping you settle in."

"Oh, that would be wonderful, dear! It was just what I was hoping you would say."

"All right, then," Elise said. "I'll get all the information we need so that we can plan our itinerary, and you can write Derrick and let him know we're coming and what day we'll be arriving."

Frieda smiled and nodded. "I'll write him as soon as we have it all planned." She sighed. "It will be so good to see my youngest son again."

Elise sent up a silent prayer asking forgiveness for being so selfish. It was only natural that her mother-in-law would want to be around her only surviving son. She'd been blessed that Frieda had stayed with her this long. And as much as she knew Frieda loved her, most probably she'd delayed moving only to help Elise with the grief they both shared when Carl had died so suddenly from apoplexy. Elise didn't know what she would have done without her.

But now it was time to quit being so selfish and let Frieda do what she wanted—and to do that, she needed help. She prayed silently, *Please, dear Lord, help me to be as giving to Frieda as she has been to me. Please help me not to show how heartsick I am over her decision. In Jesus' name I pray. Amen.*

Farmington, New Mexico Territory

After unloading the wagon of supplies he'd bought in Farmington that day, Derrick Morgan unhitched his team from the wagon and put them out to pasture. After he put up the supplies he'd left sitting on the kitchen table, he warmed up the strong coffee left over from that morning and made himself a supper of bacon and eggs. He took his plate out to his front porch and sat on the steps to eat.

Looking out over his apple orchard, he nodded and grinned. Barring bad weather, it looked as if this was going to be the best harvest he'd ever had. His trees were loaded with apples. In another month or so, he'd have people swarming over the place, helping him pick his fruit. They'd begin with the Jonathans, go on to the Delicious, then finally pick the Winesaps. It was going to be a very busy time of year, but he looked forward to it. He needed to look into getting someone to help feed the workers, but he wouldn't complain. The Lord had blessed him with a good crop, and he'd be thankful for it.

Derrick took his dishes back inside and put them in the sink along with the dishes from that morning. He poured himself another cup of coffee before lighting the lamp on the kitchen table. It was then that he pulled the letter from his mother out of his back pocket. He'd been waiting all day to open it. He'd been trying to get her to agree to move down from Denver ever since his brother, Carl, had passed away, but to no avail. He wrote her faithfully each week and looked forward to her replies even though she kept saying she needed to stay in Denver with Elise.

Elise. He sighed and shook off the thought of her. It did

no good to think of her now. Derrick opened the letter and pulled the lamp closer as he began to read:

> *My dear son,*
>   *From your last letter, it sounds as though you could use some help with your harvest. And I have been longing to see you. In light of that, I have decided to come and help with the feeding of the workers who will be picking your apples. I will be leaving here in two weeks to come to Farmington. I have included our itinerary for you. Please meet the train in Durango on the first day of September. I am counting the days until I see you again.*
>
>   *Your loving mother*

At first, pure joy that his mother was coming at long last flooded over Derrick. Then he read the letter again, and worry replaced joy. *Our* itinerary? That meant someone was coming with her. Surely if Elise was accompanying her, she would have said so. Yet who else could it be? His heart began to hammer in his chest. Would he see her again after all these years?

But what if it wasn't Elise? Maybe he should travel up there and bring his mother back. Only now wasn't a good time for him to be away for any extended time. It had to be Elise who was coming with her; surely she wouldn't let his mother travel with just anyone!

Derrick got up and paced the room. He looked at the calendar hanging by the back door. With mail being what it was here, over a week had passed since his mother had mailed this letter. She would be here in five days. There was no time to get a letter back to her. Maybe he could send a telegram to tell her he would come get her.

No. Derrick shook his head and sighed. His mother would not be pleased if he even implied that he didn't trust her to take care of herself. She'd been doing it for a long while without his help—but still. . .he didn't like the fact that he didn't know who she was traveling with! And if he asked about Elise—well, he didn't feel comfortable asking if she was coming. He'd managed to hide his feelings about her for a very long time; he certainly didn't want to raise any suspicions that he might still care.

Happiness that he would soon be seeing his mother snuck around the worry as Derrick read the letter one more time. She really was coming. She'd see how well he'd done for himself here in Farmington. He was proud of his orchard and his home. He couldn't wait for her to see them.

He looked around his kitchen. What a mess it was! Dirty dishes filled the sink, the floor needed to be swept and mopped—there was no way his home would pass his mother's inspection for cleanliness. No way at all. He went to the sink and began running water into it. There was much to do to get ready for his mother. . .and he had less than a week to do it.

❧

It hadn't been an easy trip coming down from Denver, and Elise was afraid the altitude change had been hard on her mother-in-law. They'd left Denver before dawn the day before, and at first it was exciting to watch the scenery go by. But most of it was pretty much the same in the mountains. She was getting eager to see what the country around Farmington, New Mexico Territory, was like.

They'd stopped for the noon meal at a nice hotel in Pueblo, and even by then it was a relief to get out, stretch their legs, and have a break. But the respite was over all too soon, and they boarded the train once more for the rest of what was becoming a very long day. Even though they had first-class seats, it was an extremely tiring ride as they sped along the rails.

Elise could see the weariness in her mother-in-law's eyes until finally she drifted off to sleep. She knew Frieda must be exhausted to be able to sleep with the rocking and weaving of the train car. She wished she could do the same. Instead, her mind seemed to flit from one thought to another. It was going to be so very lonely when she got back to Denver without her dear mother-in-law. Would Frieda like Farmington? How was she going to manage all alone in Denver? She wondered what Derrick would think about her traveling with his mother. Had he changed much since he'd left for New Mexico Territory over five years ago? On and on her scattered thoughts went, jumping from one subject to another.

A bend in the tracks sent Elise sliding toward the window with Frieda sliding against her, waking the older woman up.

"Oh! I must have dozed off," Frieda said. "I guess I ate too much lunch. I just could not keep my eyes open. I'm sorry, dear. I haven't been much company today."

Elise smiled at her. "I'm glad you were able to get some sleep."

"I wish you could have. How far away are we from Durango? Do you know?"

Elise shook her head. "I think we're about an hour or two out now."

Frieda looked out the window. "Look, Elise, the scenery isn't a lot different than that in Denver, is it?"

Elise shook her head. "No. But I expect it will change when we travel from Durango to where Derrick lives tomorrow."

Frieda's eyes regained a little of their natural sparkle in anticipation of seeing her son once more. "I hope Derrick received my letter telling him when to meet us."

"I'm sure he did. He'll be there. But if not, we'll just get a room at a hotel and send him a telegram."

"Oh, thank you, Elise. I'm so glad you came with me. I would probably panic if I were by myself. I haven't traveled this far in years."

"You'd do fine, Mama. But I'm glad I came, too. I'd only have worried myself sick if I hadn't."

"Now, you know what the Good Book says about worry, Elise."

"Yes, ma'am, I do. I try not to. I try to leave everything in the Lord's hands. I truly do. But I just couldn't bear the thought of you traveling this far by yourself." Elise didn't like the thought of traveling back to Denver without her, either. But she didn't say so. She didn't want Frieda to worry about her.

"Well," Frieda said, "I should take a little of my own advice. I know what the Bible says very well, yet here I am worrying about Derrick being there."

"We're a pair, aren't we?" Elise teased.

"We are that." Frieda smiled and looked out the window once again. "I'll be glad when we get to Durango. Surely we'll be there soon."

Elise did hope the trip hadn't been too much for her mother-in-law. Frieda claimed she was feeling better, but Elise had her doubts about that. She just didn't seem to have the energy she'd had a few months ago. She could only hope that her mother-in-law would perk up once they got to Farmington and were in her son's company.

two

While Derrick was thrilled that his mother was at long last coming, her timing wasn't the best. Harvesttime would be upon them soon after her arrival. He'd be too busy to show her around very much or help her get used to her new surroundings once harvest got under way.

He hoped she wouldn't mind too much. He'd been very busy the past week, checking his orchards, lining up help for harvest, and cleaning his house in preparation for his mother's arrival—and possibly that of Elise, too. He had tried to keep hope from building that he might see her again, but he wasn't doing a very good job of it. Fact of the matter was, he would love to see Elise again. He couldn't help but wonder what kind of woman she'd become.

He traveled by stage to Durango on the day before he was to meet his mother there. He booked rooms at the Strater Hotel. His mother was bound to be worn out after the train trip from Denver, and the trip on to Farmington the next day would be even more tiring for her. He couldn't wait to see her. He was eager to find out who was traveling with her and knew he would be disappointed if it wasn't Elise. Either way, from her letter, it sounded as if an extra room would be needed. If not, he could always give it up.

He spent most of the next day seeing the sights of Durango and looking at his pocket watch. Still, the day seemed to drag for him until it was time to go to the train station.

Derrick stood with a cluster of people anxiously awaiting

the train. Once they heard the whistle blow, he, along with the others, craned his neck to get the first glimpse of the locomotive as it rounded the bend and chugged into Durango.

He tried to see if he could see his mother's sweet face in one of the windows as the train slowed and came to a stop, but it was getting on toward sunset and he couldn't make out anything. Everyone on the train platform hurried forward as the conductors let down the steps of each passenger car.

Derrick's gaze went back and forth until he spotted his mother preparing to leave one of the cars. She stood there, looking all around, but he could tell she didn't see him. He hurried forward to greet her.

She spotted him just as he reached her. "Derrick! Oh, my son!"

"Mama, it is so good to see you!" His mother had aged since he'd last seen her, and she looked exhausted to him. Sudden tears sprang to the back of his eyes. To keep her from seeing how much it pained him to see her looking so frail, he hugged her to him and rocked her back and forth.

"It is so very wonderful to see you!"

His mother didn't bother to hide her tears, and Derrick hugged her again. It was only when he looked over her shoulder that he recognized the woman standing just a few feet away from them. "Elise? Is it you?"

The corners of her mouth turned up into a small smile. "Hello, Derrick. I traveled with Mama. I hope it's all right that I'm here."

"Of course it is," he answered. How could it not be all right? It was what he'd been hoping for. She was even lovelier than he remembered. Her eyes reminded him of the pond on his property, deep blue with a hint of green, and her hair appeared more red than brown in the late afternoon sunlight. She seemed a little wary, and he wondered if it was because of the trip or because of seeing him again.

"I'm sure it was a long journey getting here, and we have a ways to go by stagecoach tomorrow. I've reserved rooms for us all at the Strater. We'll have a nice dinner, and hopefully a good night's rest will ready you both for the trip home."

"A good night's rest without all that rocking and swaying over the tracks sounds wonderful," his mother said. "I still feel like I'm moving."

"If you aren't up to it tomorrow, we can wait another day, Mama," Derrick said. He hated to be away any longer than necessary, but his mother looked totally worn out, and he didn't want to tire her even more.

"I'm sure I'll be fine tomorrow, dear. I'm so eager to see your orchards. I plan on cooking for the people who help you harvest your apples."

"Mama, I didn't ask you to come live with me just so I could put you to work. Don't you worry about—"

"I know you didn't, son. But I intend to help you out as much as I can."

Derrick bent to pick up their valises. "We'll see how you feel when we get there. In the meantime, let's get you to the hotel. You can rest awhile, and then we'll get a warm meal into you."

"I certainly won't argue with that," his mother said as she and Elise followed him to the depot, where he made arrangements to have their trunks sent to the stagecoach office across the street. Then they headed down the boardwalk to the hotel.

When they reached the Strater, Derrick got their room keys from the desk clerk, and Elise and his mother followed him upstairs. Stopping at the first room, Derrick unlocked the door and glanced at Elise, who'd been very quiet on the way over. "This is your room, Elise. Mother's is right next door."

"I could stay with Mama, Derrick. There's no need for you to spend more money—"

"Of course there isn't, Derrick. Elise and I can share the same room," his mother said.

"It's all right. I didn't know for sure who was traveling with Mama, and I reserved the extra room because of that. Since I did, you might as well make use of it."

"I'll pay you—"

"I'll not hear of that, Elise," Derrick said. He knew it came out a little gruff but he hadn't meant for it to. He tried to soften his tone. "I was going to do it for a complete stranger, but I'm much happier to be doing it for you."

She gave a small smile and nodded her head. "Then I thank you."

"You're welcome." Derrick moved to the next door and unlocked it for his mother. He set her valise inside before turning back to the two women. "I'm in the room just across from you, should you need me. I've made reservations in the dining room for six o'clock. Will that be enough time for you two to freshen up?"

"That will be plenty," his mother answered.

He glanced at Elise, and she nodded. "Yes, it will be enough time."

"Good. I'll be back to escort you downstairs then." He turned to his mother and kissed her cheek. "I'm so glad you're here, Mama. Try to rest for a little while, all right? I'm going to the stage company to check on our departure time tomorrow and make sure they have your trunks." He left them both with a wave and headed back downstairs.

❧

Elise followed Frieda into her room and saw there was a connecting door to hers. "Oh, look, Mama. I can leave the door ajar in case you need me."

"That's good, Elise, dear. You may have to come wake me in about an hour. I think I'll lie down for a little while."

"I know this trip has been tiring for you. Would you like me to ask Derrick to postpone our trip to Farmington for a day or so? I'm sure he would be glad to do that for you. He's already offered."

Frieda shook her head as she sat in a chair by the window and began to unlace her shoes. "No, dear, I can't do that. He's been away from his place long enough. I'm sure he's anxious to get home with harvest coming so soon."

"All right, I'll let you rest, then." Elise was concerned about her mother-in-law. She did look exhausted. Hopefully a night of good sleep would help her. "I'll check on you in a little while." She plumped the pillows on the bed and kissed Frieda's cheek before going to her room.

She was tempted to take a nap herself but was afraid they'd both oversleep and not be ready when Derrick came to get them. So she sat in the chair and looked out over the street instead. She'd been a little taken aback by her reaction to seeing Derrick. For some reason her heart seemed to have taken wings and fluttered against her ribs, and she wasn't sure why.

He'd aged some since she'd seen him last, just as she had. But the lines around his eyes served to make him seem more mature than his age, and Elise thought he was even better looking than she'd remembered. He and Carl had never looked much alike—Carl had looked more like his mother, while Derrick took after his father. Carl's hair had been sandy and his eyes brown. Derrick's hair was almost black, now with a few silver strands beginning to show, and his eyes were deep blue. He was taller than Carl had been, too. So her reaction to him wasn't because he reminded her of Carl, and that fact discomfited Elise most of all.

She hadn't been able to tell how he felt about her being here. He'd been very cordial to her, but Frieda had taught her sons good manners, and she knew Derrick wouldn't let her know if he was upset about her arrival. She should have asked Frieda why she hadn't told Derrick whom she was traveling with, but she'd forgotten to when they were alone, and she guessed it really didn't matter now. She wouldn't be here long anyway—only long enough to see that her mother-in-law was settled in.

Elise spent the next half hour straightening her valise and freshening up. She took her hair down, brushed it until it shone, and then pulled it up and back into a knot on the top of her head. She looked at the small pendant watch pinned to her lapel and saw that it was time to wake Frieda.

She knocked lightly on the connecting door and was a little surprised when Frieda opened the door with a hairbrush in her hand. "Did you not get any rest, Mama?"

"I tried but was too excited, I suppose." Frieda continued to brush her hair as she spoke. "So I just got up and freshened up for dinner. I'm sure I'll sleep quite well tonight. The bed is good."

Elise hoped Frieda would sleep well, because even through her excitement about being here, she looked very tired. "You just look weary, Mama. I do hope this trip hasn't been too much for you."

"It hasn't. I'll retire early tonight and be fine tomorrow. You'll see," Frieda assured her once more.

Elise sent up a silent prayer that her mother-in-law was right. They still had a long way to go tomorrow, and the stage would be much more uncomfortable than the train had been. "I hope so."

Elise took the brush from Frieda. "Let me do your hair. You know you love to have it brushed."

"Thank you, dear. You have such a nice touch with my hair. I'll certainly miss you dressing it for me when you go back to Denver."

Elise would miss it, too. She brushed her mother-in-law's long silver hair and then dressed it much the same as she had her own. She pulled it up and back and twisted it into a loose knot at the top of Frieda's head. "There. You look lovely. Are you hungry?"

"I am. And I'm looking forward to seeing my son again. He's changed a great deal in the last few years, don't you think?"

"He does seem more—"

"Mature," Frieda said, nodding as she finished Elise's sentence. "I think he's come into his own as a man."

There came a knock on the door, and Frieda crossed the room, opening it to her son. Elise's heart did a little jig as she saw Derrick standing there looking even more handsome than he had that afternoon. He was clean shaven, his hair was neatly parted just slightly left of center, and his coat looked as if he'd just brushed it.

His face lit up in a smile for his mother. "Are you hungry? My stomach is growling at the aromas drifting up the staircase."

Frieda stuck her head out into the hall. "Something smells quite good. And yes, I believe I could eat a bite. Elise, dear, are you ready?"

"I am." She followed her mother-in-law out into the hall. The aromas wafting up the staircase did indeed smell wonderful.

"Well, let's go down. Derrick, you always did have a good appetite."

Derrick crooked an elbow for his mother to take, and Elise followed the two of them down the staircase. Tired as she must be, Frieda looked very happy to be with her son, and Elise couldn't help but be glad she'd come.

They were shown to a table in front of a window overlooking the street, and Elise felt quite comfortable listening to mother and son catch up with each other while they waited for their meal to be served. They weren't disappointed in it. Their supper was every bit as tasty as they'd hoped it would be. The fried chicken was crisp and tender. It was served with mashed potatoes, gravy, and fluffy biscuits. For dessert they had their choice of chocolate cake or cherry pie.

Throughout the meal, Derrick described his orchard and told them of his hopes for the future. "I have one of the larger orchards in the area," he said with a hint of pride in his voice. "The trees are full of apples, and that means I need a lot of help picking them during harvest. Then they're packed and shipped by overland freight here to Durango and then out by rail. I've been working hard to line up buyers for my apples over the last few years. By the time the railroad line finally makes it to Farmington, I hope to have Morgan Orchards firmly established. Shipping by train will make things much easier, and the apples will get to market much earlier. The ground here is so fertile, I think Farmington is going to be a major farming community in the future. And I'm hoping to be a large part of it."

"I am so very proud of you, son," Frieda said. "Your papa

would be, too. I can't wait to see your place."

Elise found that she couldn't wait, either.

❧

Derrick couldn't help but notice that Elise watched his mother as closely as he did while the stage jostled its passengers this way and that on its journey to Farmington. It seemed that with each passing mile, his mother looked paler and more exhausted.

He couldn't have been more relieved when they stopped for a meal at the halfway station. Maybe the brief break from all the jostling would help his mother. Derrick helped her down from the stage, then gave Elise a hand down while steadying his mother with his free arm until she could get used to solid ground once more.

The meal wasn't great, but Derrick was proud that Elise and his mother ate it as if it were, while others at the table groused about the quality of the food. Finally the driver told the grumblers that they could wait outside if the food wasn't up to their standards. That quieted them right down.

By the time they boarded the stage once more, Derrick was just glad that the next stop would be Farmington. He sat beside his mother, hoping that if she were able to get a nap, she would feel comfortable leaning her head against his shoulder. The meal must have helped some, or maybe it was the boredom of seeing mile after mile of the same scenery pass by that had his mother falling asleep only a few miles out from the way station. Derrick eased an arm around her to help steady her in her slumber and could have kicked himself for not staying one more night in Durango.

He glanced across at Elise and found that her attention was on his mother. When she shifted her gaze and saw him looking at her, she smiled. He wanted to ask Elise about his mother's health. He had gone to her door first last evening, hoping to have a talk with her, but she'd been in his mother's room. It wouldn't have seemed proper to knock on her door after his mother retired for the evening. And there was no time this morning, as they were rushing around to catch the stage on time.

There was not even a chance to talk now, with the stage full of passengers and his mother asleep on his shoulder. Conversation with Elise would have to wait until they could have a moment alone.

three

By the time the stage reached Farmington, it was almost suppertime. Derrick took his mother and Elise to one of the hotel restaurants to eat before heading home. There was no way he would expect either of them to prepare a meal as tired as they both looked. After they ate, he left them in the lobby to rest while he went to the stage company and loaded his mother's trunks and the rest of their bags onto the buckboard he'd left in town.

He went back to pick them up, and as he headed for home, even though his orchard was only a few miles out of town, Derrick suspected it felt like a hundred to the two women. The sun was just setting when he turned onto the road that led to his place. Derrick could tell just by looking at the two women that they were exhausted. But they were troupers and tried not to show it, exclaiming over the beautiful sunset and the size of his orchard as he pulled the wagon up in front of his house. It was a two-story white frame house that gleamed in the last rays of sunlight.

"Oh, son, what a wonderful place you have here," his mother said as he jumped down and turned to lift her to the ground.

"Thank you, Mama." He gave Elise a hand down and led them to the front porch. "Come on inside. I'll show you around the house, then bring in your things."

He unlocked the door and stood aside so that both women could enter the parlor. As Derrick led them through the dining room and into the kitchen, he was rewarded by the oohs and aahs he heard as they followed him though the house.

"I'll put the kettle on for some tea for you, Mama."

"Thank you, son," she said, nodding as she looked around the room. He could tell she liked it, but he couldn't take a lot of credit for the home's furnishings. The previous owner had sold it to him furnished. She had told him she'd ordered the newest range from Sears & Roebuck just six months before selling the place. Nothing in the house was very old, and he had a feeling she'd furnished the whole house by ordering out of the catalog. He was glad his mother and Elise seemed to like it all.

"Oh, Derrick, I don't know what I expected, but this is all even nicer than I'd thought it would be." His mother turned to him and chuckled as she watched him fill the teakettle. "And I *never* expected that you'd have running water in the kitchen! That will make cooking for your extra hands much easier during harvest."

Derrick couldn't wait to see her reaction to the biggest surprise he had for her. "I'm glad you like it, Mama," he said, kissing her on the cheek. "While we're waiting for the water to boil, let me show you upstairs if you're up to it. Then I'll bring in your things while you and Elise relax with a cup of tea."

"Of course I'm up to it. Lead the way," his mother said with a smile.

Derrick explained more about his home as they went upstairs. "I've done a few things to the place, but I have to admit it was in pretty good shape when I bought it."

"Why would anyone want to sell it?"

"Well, the owner was a widow, and after her husband died, she wanted to take her children back east. I just heard about it at the right time. She was selling it completely furnished so that she didn't have to ship everything back all that way. I made her a fair offer, and she took it. So I had a lot to work with."

"That was the Lord working for you, son."

Derrick felt a twinge of guilt at the reminder of all the Lord had provided for him since he'd moved to New Mexico Territory. He hadn't acknowledged it often enough. "I'm sure you're right, Mama."

He reached the landing and walked down the hall to the room facing the front of his property. "This room will be yours, Mama. I hope you like it."

It had been furnished with a matching bedstead, washstand, and dresser of solid oak. The cream-colored wallpaper was covered with pink and red rosebud vines. The bed coverings looked as if they'd been made to match.

"Oh, Derrick, this is lovely. I love the colors."

"I remembered that red is one of your favorites. You can have any room in the house for your own, but I thought this just fit you."

"It's perfect, dear."

Derrick led the way back out into the hall and opened the door across the way. "I hope this room will be all right for you, Elise. They had several daughters, so both rooms were decorated with girls in mind."

This room also had matching furniture but was decorated in soft yellows. "This is very nice, Derrick. I'm sure I'll be quite comfortable here until I go back to Denver. Thank you."

That was the first mention of her returning to Denver, and Derrick wasn't sure how he felt about it. Seeing the expression on his mother's face, he wasn't sure how she felt about it, either.

"Where is your room, dear?" his mother asked.

"It's at the other end of the hallway. It's done in blue and white. Come and see." Derrick led the way to his room and opened the door, glad that he had made his own bed before leaving for Durango.

"Oh, I like this, too. And I can see why you chose it." Frieda chuckled. "No flowers."

"I'm sure she decorated it with her husband in mind," Derrick said. "I like flowers, but the striped paper suits my taste much better."

"What is this room?" Elise asked as they turned back into the hall.

"Open it and see," Derrick said. "I saved the best for last."

"Ohhh, a bathroom—with running water," his mother said. "We can take real baths, Elise!"

Derrick had been watching Elise's reaction closely, all the while trying not to show how much it mattered to him. He breathed an inward sigh of relief when a huge smile spread across her face.

"This is very nice. And it's very big. Was this here when you bought the house, Derrick?" Elise asked.

"No. Getting running water to the house was my job." And he was very proud of it. He'd worked hard the year before to get the windmill running and then get running water up to the house installed. Now, as he saw the expressions on the two women's faces, Derrick was doubly glad that he could at least offer them a private place with a tub to bathe in.

"This was an extra room, probably meant as a nursery, although the owner had a sewing machine set up in it. Her husband had bought the fixtures and had planned on doing it all. I couldn't see not going on with it."

"Well, you'll be glad to know that we appreciate your hard

work very much. We'll be making good use of it, son!"

Derrick laughed. "I figured you might." The teakettle began to sing from downstairs. "Let's get you some tea, and I'll bring in your things so you can get settled in."

❧

Elise followed Derrick and Frieda back to the kitchen. His home was really lovely, and when she left she'd feel better knowing that Frieda had all the modern conveniences she'd become accustomed to in Denver. She hadn't expected it to be this nice. Oh, it needed a few personal touches here and there—although all the furnishings were very nice, it needed the smell of home-cooked meals, the sound of laughter, and the closeness of family to make it feel warm and welcoming. But it was a house that would be a joy to make into a home, and she was sure Frieda would enjoy going about doing just that—once she rested.

Derrick pulled a teapot out of his cupboard. "I'll let you two make your tea the way you like it while I bring in your things."

Frieda started to pull down cups from the cupboard, but Elise gently turned her away. "Mama, let me do this. You go sit at the table and I'll bring it to you."

"Thank you, dear," Frieda said with a sigh.

Elise and Derrick exchanged looks before he went to get their bags. If either of them had needed any convincing as to how tired Frieda was, her words and her shuffle over to the table told it all.

Elise had been watching Frieda carefully over the past few days. She wasn't sure how her mother-in-law could be much help to Derrick during harvest if she didn't get to feeling better. Elise didn't think she could go back to Denver with Frieda so worn out.

She made the tea and sweetened Frieda's just as she liked it before taking it over to place it in front of her. "I'm afraid this trip has tired you more than we thought it would, Mama."

"I'll be fine, dear. I just need a bath and a good night's sleep, then I'll be back to normal. You'll see."

She'd said much the same thing the night before. But Elise had her doubts as she saw her mother-in-law's hand shake slightly when she brought her cup to her mouth. She didn't voice them, however. Instead, she said, "I hope so. I'll run you a bath after you finish your tea and unpack your nightgown and robe."

"That sounds wonderful, dear. I can't wait to try out that nice feather bed upstairs. I am so happy for Derrick. His papa and Carl would be so proud of him."

"That they would," Elise agreed, suddenly feeling a twinge of guilt when she realized she hadn't thought of Carl once since she'd been here at Derrick's home. And it was the day before that she'd been thinking about how different they looked. . . .

She could hear Derrick's footsteps on the stairs as he took up their baggage, and in only moments he was back down in the kitchen. "I've put everything in your rooms. If you need anything, just let me know, all right?" He sat down at the table and grinned at his mother. "I still can't believe you're here, Mama. But I'm afraid the trip has worn you out. Please sleep in and rest up tomorrow."

Frieda looked from Derrick to Elise and shook her head at the two of them. "Don't worry about me. I'll admit that I am a little tired. I'm not as young as I used to be, after all. But a night or two of good sleep will fix me up and I'll be fine." She took a sip of tea and then chuckled. "I'm just glad I don't have to get back on that train or on that stagecoach tomorrow."

"If I had to pick one, it would have to be the train," Elise offered. "I only *thought* it was uncomfortable, but it was nothing like the stage!"

"I hate that you'll have to ride it again, Elise, dear."

"Oh, I'll be fine, Mama. And the train will be on the last leg of the trip." But she didn't want to think about leaving just yet. It was going to be awfully lonely back in Denver with no one but herself for company.

"Well, there's certainly no hurry for you to leave. You both need to rest after your journey here," Derrick said. "I've got to tend to some things out in the barn, so I'll tell you good night now. I hope you both sleep well."

"I'm sure we will, son."

Derrick kissed his mother on the cheek. "See you tomorrow. Good night, Mama. Good night, Elise."

After Derrick left, Elise ran up to lay out Frieda's nightclothes and run her bathwater. Once she had the older woman upstairs and soaking in the tub, she went back down to straighten up the kitchen. She rinsed out the teakettle and washed the teapot, cups, and saucers. Even if Frieda was up in the morning, Elise planned to be down to help her fix breakfast for Derrick. It was the least she could do to repay his hospitality.

She looked in the pantry beside the back porch to find it well stocked with staples. She found the coffee and went back upstairs feeling confident that she could put together a meal for him.

Frieda had just come back from the bathroom, and Elise turned down her bed for her. "I certainly hope you feel better in the morning, Mama. But don't worry about breakfast for Derrick. I'll make it for him if you aren't up to it."

"Thank you, dear. I'm sure I will be. It is so good to finally be here. You aren't going back right away, are you, Elise?"

"I won't be going anywhere until I know you've recovered from the trip, Mama."

Frieda yawned as she sat down on the bed and slipped under the covers. "Thank you so much for coming with me, dear. The trip would have been much harder if you hadn't." Her eyes were closed as soon as her head hit the pillow. " 'Night, dear."

Elise kissed her on the cheek. "Good night, Mama."

She turned out the lamp on the bedside table and went to take her own bath. She couldn't wait to sink into her own bed.

As Elise ran her water, she couldn't help but be touched by Derrick's thoughtfulness to his mother. He'd provided bath salts and soft Turkish toweling for her comfort. There were other towels in the linen closet. Elise doubted that Derrick used the softer ones, figuring he'd bought them for his mother. She felt selfish all over again for keeping Frieda to herself for so long.

As she soaked in the warm water and let the travel weariness ease away, she wondered why Derrick had never married. He was handsome and obviously could provide well. Surely there were women in the area who would be honored to be his wife. Of course there were. But for some reason that thought didn't really sit well with Elise, and she didn't want to delve into why. She hurriedly finished her bath, then drained the tub. It really wasn't any of her business why he'd never married anyway.

Elise straightened up the bathroom and peeked in on Frieda. She was snoring lightly, so Elise went to her room, relieved that her mother-in-law seemed to be sleeping soundly. She went to the window and looked out. Evidently Derrick was still in the barn. She could see a dim light shining from inside.

He was probably staying out there so as not to run into the two of them getting ready for bed. She hoped he really didn't mind that she'd come with his mother. Family was one thing, but she was really only related to him by marriage, and they'd not really been around each other much after she and Carl married. Derrick had moved away a few months later.

She remembered him from before Carl began courting her. At one time, Elise had hoped Derrick would be the one to ask to court her. But it was his brother instead, and she'd never regretted marrying Carl. He had been a wonderful husband, and she missed him. She missed being married and having someone to care for. Elise sighed. She'd been blessed to have him for the time she did, and she certainly didn't need to start feeling sorry for herself now.

She went to the bed and knelt down to say her prayers. "Dear Lord, I thank You for seeing Mama and me safely here. Please let her sleep well tonight and feel rested tomorrow. Please help me to know what to do, whether to stay here awhile to help out or go back to Denver. It's going to be so very lonely there, Father. Please help me not to show how badly I'm dreading going back by myself. It's Derrick's turn to have his mother with him. I'm sure he's been lonely all these years without family nearby. Please help me to remember that. Thank You for all my many blessings, Father. And thank You most of all for Your precious Son and our Savior, Jesus Christ. In His name I pray. Amen."

She plumped her pillow and got into bed, sighing with relief as her body felt the softness of the mattress.

≈

Derrick put up his wagon, then took care of his horses, feeding them and putting them up for the night. He checked on his barn animals, thankful for his neighbor, Jed Barrister, who'd milked his cow while he was gone. They took turns looking after each other's places when they were away—which wasn't very often—and would help each other with their harvests.

He was a little unsettled about how good it felt to see Elise and his mother in his kitchen. Well, not about seeing his mother there, but Elise. When he'd first moved into the house, he'd dreamed of Elise there in that very kitchen, but she was his brother's wife. Through the years he'd forced thoughts of her to the back of his mind. Only now, his brother was no longer here and Elise was. It was difficult not to think of her when she was there in his house—the setting of many a dream about her. It was also impossible to ignore the pounding of his heart when she smiled at him. But he had to try. She was his brother's widow, after all.

He busied himself for over an hour so that his mother and Elise would have some privacy while they got ready for bed. By the time he finally headed back to the house, he was pretty sure they had turned in for the night. There was only a light shining from the kitchen window and none upstairs. He hoped they both slept well.

He still hadn't talked to Elise about his mother. He'd have to find a way tomorrow. Elise needed her rest, too. She'd looked almost as tired as his mother tonight. Hopefully that meant it was only the travel that had his mother looking so frail and she would be better after a little rest.

He hoped Elise would stay awhile, telling himself it would make it easier on his mother. He could tell she would miss Elise a great deal. Maybe he'd been wrong to insist that she come and live with him instead of with his brother's wife.

As he stepped into the kitchen from his porch, he realized the room had a different feel to it tonight. The kitchen might be empty, but the house wasn't. Suddenly Derrick realized how very lonely he'd been the last few years. He loved his place and the work he did, but at night when he had no one to share it all with, the solitude could be hard to take. He sent up a silent prayer, thanking the Lord above for seeing his mother and Elise safely to his home.

four

Derrick awakened early, dressed quickly, and hurried into the bathroom as quietly as he could to wash his face and shave. Had his mother and Elise not been there, the shaving might have waited another day, but having women in the house necessitated sprucing up a bit, and he wanted to do it before they needed to get in the bathroom. He really didn't mind. It was nice to have a reason to do so.

He went downstairs as quietly as he could, so as not to awaken the women, and went out to the barn to milk old Bessie. He loved this quiet time of morning when the sun was coming up over the horizon. He took the warm pail of milk and the fresh eggs he'd collected to the kitchen, and then went back out to feed his chickens and take care of the other farm animals.

When he came back to the house, the smell of brewing coffee and frying bacon wafted out to greet him. His mother must have slept well, or not at all, to be up already. He certainly hoped she was up so early because she'd slept well.

He took the back steps two at a time, entering the kitchen expecting to see his mother standing at the stove. Instead, it was Elise who turned to him with a smile. His heart thudded against his chest, and his pulse began to race. He nearly pinched himself to make sure he was awake.

"Good morning, Derrick. I wanted to get down here before Mama tried to. I hope it's all right that I made myself at home in your kitchen?"

It was more than all right. It was something right out of his dreams. "Of course it is. It's been a very long time since I've had anyone cook breakfast for me—and never here."

She took the last of the bacon out of the skillet and cracked a couple of eggs into a bowl. "How do you want your eggs cooked?"

"Over easy, if it's not too much trouble." He still couldn't quite accept that Elise was here, in his kitchen, cooking for him. "Is Mama all right this morning?"

"I think so. She seemed to be sleeping soundly when I checked on her, and I didn't want to disturb her. So I just let her sleep." Elise slid the eggs into the frying pan she'd just taken the last of the bacon from.

Derrick nodded and poured himself a cup of the coffee he was sure was much better than what he made. "I'm glad she's resting. I'm sure she can use the sleep. She seemed so very tired last night. I've wanted to ask you about her health. I must admit I didn't expect her to look quite so frail."

"She'd been feeling a little poorly for a few months before she decided to come here, but she seemed to perk up as we got ready for the trip. I have a feeling she was only acting as if she felt better, though, knowing I didn't want her to travel until she was up to it. That's why I came with her. I couldn't bear the thought of her traveling by herself." She turned the eggs over and then bent to take a pan of biscuits out of the oven.

"Thank you, Elise. I appreciate your care of her more than I can say. And I know she's going to miss you very much when you do return to Denver."

"Not nearly as much as I will miss her."

"Is there anything pressing that you need to get back to Denver for?" Derrick asked. He thought his brother had left her well off enough that she didn't have to worry about income. He hoped so, anyway.

Elise shook her head as she flipped the two eggs onto a plate and added a good portion of bacon to the side along with a couple of hot biscuits. "No."

Derrick's mouth began to water at the aroma drifting up from the plate he took from her. "Would you consider staying on until we're sure Mama's health improves?"

"Of course I will. And thank you for asking me to stay on until then. I would be miserable worrying about her if I went home with her still feeling poorly." She put a biscuit and a few pieces of bacon on a plate and joined him at the table. "Would you say the blessing, please?"

Derrick was thankful he hadn't already popped half a biscuit into his mouth. Praying before meals wasn't something he was used to doing, living by himself. Thankful he hadn't embarrassed himself, he nodded and bowed his head. "Dear Lord, thank You for safe travel for Mama and Elise. Please help Mama to feel better soon. Thank You for all of our blessings. And thank You for this food we are about to eat. In Jesus' name I pray. Amen."

"Thank you," Elise said as she buttered her biscuit.

By the time she broke off a piece and put it in her mouth, Derrick had eaten a whole biscuit. She was every bit as good a cook as his mother was.

"There you two are," Derrick's mother said as she entered the kitchen, looking a little more rested than she had the day before. "Elise, dear, you should have awakened me."

"You needed the rest, Mama," Elise said, jumping up to make a plate for his mother. "Sit down at the table. I'll fix yours."

"I am perfectly capable of waiting on myself, dear."

"I know you are. But when I go back to Denver, I won't be able to do this for you, so please. . .let me wait on you now." She cracked an egg into the skillet and quickly scrambled it for his mother.

"Just for today," Frieda said as she took a seat at the table. "I can't let you spoil me too much. Harvest will be here, and I need to be in top form to be of help to Derrick."

"Mama, I can hire someone to cook for the hands. It's what I would do if you hadn't come." Derrick was afraid all the extra work would be much too hard for her.

"I'll be fine. When is harvest?"

"In a few weeks, but—"

"Why, that's lots of time. I'll be up to the task by then. I don't want you paying someone for what I can easily do."

Elise brought his mother's plate and a cup of coffee to her. Derrick's glance met hers across the top of his mother's head, but neither of them said what they were thinking. Derrick only knew what he was hoping—that his mother would get better, but that Elise would stay on even after she did.

His mother broke into his thoughts. "What time is church tomorrow, son?"

Derrick had to think. He hadn't been going like he should, but he knew what time it started because the preacher had ridden out to see him several weeks before to remind him of it. "Ten o'clock. That's to give those who live out a ways time to get into town."

"We'll need to press a few things before then. You do have an iron, don't you, son?"

"Yes, ma'am, I do. It's in the pantry."

"I saw it earlier," Elise said. "I'll get everything pressed as soon as we finish up breakfast. And I'll help you unpack your trunk later today, Mama."

"Thank you, dear. There's no hurry to unpack everything, though. We just need to make sure we have things ready for tomorrow. Do you have a good preacher here, Derrick?"

The way his mother was quizzing him, Derrick couldn't help but wonder if she knew he hadn't been attending like he should have. He had heard reports from friends and neighbors on the preacher, though, and could honestly say, "Everyone around here thinks so."

"I look forward to hearing him. . .and to meeting your friends and neighbors."

"After breakfast, I'm going to run to the farm across the way and thank my neighbor for taking care of things while I was in Durango. Would you two like to ride with me?" Derrick asked his mother.

"I'd love to. Elise, you'll come along, too, won't you?"

❧

Elise didn't know what to say. She was already feeling much too comfortable here. She would have to go back to Denver at some point, and the more she came to feel settled here, the more she might hate going back. Besides, Derrick and his mother had not had any time alone.

"I think I'll stay here, thanks. I'll use the time to press our clothes and clean up the kitchen."

"I'll help clean up—"

Elise shook her head. "No, Mama. You and Derrick need some time together, and these will be your new neighbors, too. You need to get to know them. You two go on and have a lovely day."

"But—"

"Mama, I'll hitch up the wagon after I finish this cup of coffee and be back to pick you up," Derrick said, ending any argument his mother might have had.

Elise was grateful. She was having enough problems trying to figure out her confused feelings about being in Derrick's home as it was. She couldn't see how spending more time in his company would help her sort them out.

Derrick got up from the table and took his dishes to the sink. "Thank you for breakfast, Elise. I don't normally eat that well."

"You're welcome. I'm glad you enjoyed it. Your kitchen is a pleasure to cook in."

"Thank you. I didn't show you the root cellar last night, but it's right under the pantry. Just raise the door in the pantry floor and use the handrail on the stairs. There's a hook at the bottom to hang a lantern. I'll be going into Farmington for supplies on Monday. If there's anything you and Mama think I need, just make a list. You're both welcome to go with me into town."

"I'll check it out while you're gone. If you have any salt pork and beans, I can put some of those on for supper. I can make some gravy to go with the leftover biscuits for dinner, too."

"Anything you want to do is fine with me," Derrick said on his way out the door.

"I'll help you when we get back, Elise, dear," Frieda said. "I'm just anxious to see Derrick's place and see what this country looks like. It's far different than Denver, that's for sure."

"It is. I love the mountains in Colorado, but there are so many trees, the views of the sunsets and sunrises are sometimes blocked," Elise said. "This part of the country is so wide open—just the high mesas here and there and not many trees to block the views. I don't think I've ever seen a more beautiful sunrise than the one this morning. And you can see the river from upstairs. I know you're going to love it here. You go and enjoy your time with Derrick, Mama. Get to know your new neighbors."

Frieda smiled and brought her plate to the sink, where Elise had begun to wash dishes. "I think I will."

It didn't take long before Derrick was back to pick up his mother. Elise breathed a sigh of relief when the wagon pulled away. She needed a little time to herself, if for no other reason than to sort out her feelings. Part of her wanted to resent Derrick for pulling Frieda away from Denver. The other part of her felt bad that it'd been so long since Frieda and her son had seen each other. And he was so obviously happy to have his mother here.

When Derrick first entered the kitchen and smiled at her this morning, Elise was sure he'd been expecting to see his mother, so the smile had probably been for her. But it had lit up his whole face and stayed there even after he'd found her, not his mother, at the stove.

Her heart had fluttered like a caged bird in her chest at that smile. She wasn't sure what that was all about, nor did she want to think about it now. She wanted to be happy for Derrick and his mother's reunion—and she was. It was only the thought of going back to Denver alone that put a damper on her joy for them.

She was thankful for the extra time Derrick had extended to her in his request for her to stay until Frieda was her old self again. Yet in the long run, Elise had a feeling it would only make it more difficult to say good-bye.

⋅⋅

After another of Elise's breakfasts—this one of ham and gravy and biscuits—Derrick took his mother and Elise to church the next morning. He hoped no one would mention how long it had been since they'd last seen him there, because it had been quite awhile. When he first moved to Farmington, he'd meant to come regularly. Instead, he had only attended sporadically the last several years, and he had a feeling his mother was about to find that out.

Several church members he'd never met came up to welcome them and introduce themselves.

Then one of his neighbors came up to him. "Good to see you here, Derrick," Eli Johnson said to him. "It's been awhile."

Derrick cringed inside but only replied, "Good to see you, too, Eli."

After several others had come up and told him how glad they were to see him, Derrick had a feeling from the look his mother shot him that he'd be hearing a word or two when services were over.

But as the service got under way, Derrick realized that he'd missed coming. Peacefulness settled inside him as he sat between his mother and Elise, and it was only then that he came to realize that maybe he'd been a little angry with the Lord over letting Carl win the woman he'd wanted for himself.

Harold Burton preached a good sermon on forgiveness, and Derrick knew the message was meant for him. As he joined in the closing song with the rest of the congregation, he sent up a silent prayer. He asked the Lord to help him forgive Carl once and for all and to forgive *him* for his anger at a brother who was no longer here. He also asked the Lord to forgive him for not making more of an effort to come to church and be part of the body as he knew he should have.

When the service was over, more people came up to him, his mother, and Elise on the way out of the building. Now he was certain he'd be doing a lot of explaining to his mother.

Preacher Burton was standing at the door, along with his

wife, Rachel. Derrick didn't think they were much older than he was, but they seemed wise beyond their years. The two men shook hands.

"Derrick, it's good to see you here. We've missed you. Who are these two lovely ladies you have with you?"

Derrick made the introductions. "This is my mother, Frieda Morgan, and my sister-in-law, Elise Morgan. Mother, Elise, this is our preacher, Harold Burton, and his wife, Rachel Burton."

"I enjoyed your lesson a great deal," his mother said.

"Thank you. It's always nice to hear that," Harold replied

"It's very nice to have you with us today," Rachel said. "Will you be staying long?"

"Mama is moving here to live with me."

"And Elise came to help me get settled in," his mother added.

"How wonderful! It's always good to have more women in town. I hope we'll see more of you in the weeks to come."

"Oh yes," his mother said. "We'll be here next week."

"Good." Rachel smiled and nodded at Frieda.

After a little more small talk, Derrick escorted his mother and Elise to the wagon, then helped them up onto the seats. As he turned the wagon, heading it for home, he half expected his mother to say something about his not going to church like he should.

But all she said was, "It's a nice church, and the people are very friendly. I look forward to going next week."

"Yes, it seems a good congregation. And the singing was beautiful," Elise added.

As the two women got into a discussion about the church service, Derrick breathed a sigh of relief. He knew how his mother felt about attending church, and she was right. He deserved whatever she might have to say. But it wasn't until he went with her and Elise this morning that he realized why he'd stopped attending.

Elise and he were the same age, and she had made his heart beat faster for at least a year before his older brother began courting her. It was his own fault that Carl won her heart. He should have acted faster. But he hadn't, and when Elise had accepted Carl's marriage proposal, it had hurt badly. But what had hurt the most was that Carl had never shown an interest in Elise until he found out that Derrick was attracted to her. It had felt like a betrayal to Derrick.

But all that was in the past, Derrick told himself. He needed to keep it there. Carl was gone and Elise was his widow. There was no good in harboring resentment toward a man who wasn't here to defend himself—especially when the man was his brother.

But Derrick knew he could get very accustomed to seeing Elise in his kitchen each morning. He was even more attracted to her now than he had been in Denver. She'd gone from a pretty young girl to a lovely woman, and from the care she showed his mother, he knew she'd kept the sweetness about her.

He was still attracted to her. There was no doubt about that. And the biggest problem with having her here was that he didn't know how he was going to be able to live in the same house with his mother and Elise without giving away how he felt. But even more troublesome—when it was time for her to return to Denver, how was he going to be able to handle losing her once more?

five

The next morning when Derrick came down for breakfast, Elise was at the range frying bacon as usual, but her normally smooth brow was slightly furrowed.

"What's wrong, Elise? You look worried. Is Mama all right?"

"She developed a slight cough overnight," Elise said as she poured a cup of coffee and handed it to him. "Is there a doctor in town she could see? It sounds much like the cough she had in Denver when she felt so bad, and I am a little concerned."

"There's Doc Bedslow. I'm sure he will see her. I was planning on going into town for supplies today anyway. I'll take her along if she's up to it. If not, I'll get him to come out here."

He heard his mother cough on her way down the stairs, and he didn't like the sound of it any better than Elise did.

Elise brought a cup of coffee with cream and sugar to the table for her.

"Thank you, dear," his mother said just before she coughed again.

"Mama, I'm going into town, and I want you to ride with me if you're up to it. I want you to let Doc Bedslow listen to your chest."

"No," Frieda protested, "I'll be fine. I've had this before, and—"

"And I'm afraid you never quite got over it, Mama. You need to see a doctor," Elise said.

"If it's nothing, you can scold me, Mama," Derrick said. "I'd like to think that you could just still be tired from the trip. But neither of us like the sound of that cough, and I know I'd find it hard to forgive myself for not getting you to a doctor if you have some underlying illness that needs to be taken care of."

"I feel the same way, Mama," Elise added.

"You need to see the doctor, Mama," Derrick insisted. "If you don't feel like riding into town, I'll have the doctor come out here."

His mother sighed deeply and shook her head. "No, that won't be necessary. I'll go into town with you."

Elise helped his mother get ready to go after they finished breakfast, and she rode along with them. Derrick wasn't sure if it was for his mother's sake or his own, but he was certainly glad she was there.

They didn't have to wait too long for Dr. Bedslow to see her. After listening to her chest and checking her out, he told them that it appeared she had a slight case of pneumonia. "After talking to your mother, Derrick, I'm pretty sure she's had a relapse. She said she'd been feeling poorly before she came down here from Denver. Her resistance hadn't been up enough for the trip, and it probably set her back a week or so. *If* she takes her medicine, rests, and lets herself heal, she should be back to normal in a few weeks."

"We'll see that she does that. Thanks, Doc."

They were relieved that Frieda could regain her health and strength. But both Derrick and Elise took turns blaming themselves as they all left the doctor's office with a prescription for his mother's cough.

"I should have gotten you to the doctor up in Denver, Mama. I am so sorry."

"You tried to get me to go, Elise, dear. I stubbornly refused."

"Well, I shouldn't have kept insisting you make that long

trip down here," Derrick said. "Or at the very least, I should have insisted you stop along the way and spend a night in a hotel. It might have taken longer for you to get here, but you wouldn't have been so worn out."

"Derrick, dear, it isn't your fault, either. I have a mind of my own and I wanted to come when I did. I truly thought I was better, and I didn't realize how tiring the trip would be for me. I'll take it easy and regain my strength. I promise. After all, I'm not much good if I can't help you out."

"Mother! You don't have to do anything around the house. I just wanted you here. I didn't ask you to come so that I would have a cook or a maid!"

Frieda nodded. "I know that, dear. I didn't mean that the way it sounded. I just want to help you out."

"You're helping me more than you know just by being here. Don't ever doubt that. Now, let me buy you two dinner and then we'll go get our supplies. But when we get home, Mama, you must take a nap."

He waited for an argument from her, and even Elise looked as if she were holding her breath waiting for the same thing, but none was forthcoming. Instead, all his mother said was, "Yes, dear."

❧

During the next few days, Elise took it on herself to unpack her mother-in-law's trunks. With Frieda's instructions on where to put things, Derrick's house began to look like home. Her mother-in-law had brought family pictures and favorite knickknacks she'd had packed away since moving in with Elise and Carl. Elise arranged them here and there in the parlor and other rooms in the house and hung some of the pictures along the wall next to the staircase. Frieda's tea service seemed meant for the sideboard in the dining room. Derrick seemed pleased with the additions to his home, noticing each new thing that was put out.

They'd settled into somewhat of a routine, with Elise up early and preparing breakfast before Derrick went out to check his orchards and do chores. For the first few days after they saw the doctor, Frieda stayed in bed, and Elise or Derrick took meals up to her. But it didn't take long for her to tire of being in bed all day, so Elise and Derrick agreed that she could come down after her afternoon nap and stay until after supper if she felt like it.

In between meals and before starting supper, Elise would dust and straighten up. Frieda claimed she was feeling better, and Elise knew she wanted to be. But Elise still wasn't sure her mother-in-law was up to the task of all she wanted to do for Derrick—not if he started harvesting those apples anytime soon.

Elise had come to love the smell of Derrick's orchards. There was a big apple tree just outside the back door of the kitchen, and she loved to sit under it at times throughout the day, coffee or tea in hand, and just enjoy the beauty and aroma of this new place.

On this day, Elise decided to surprise Frieda and Derrick. Taking her cup inside, she grabbed a basket and went back out to the tree. She picked just enough of the ripest-looking apples from the lower branches to make a pie for dessert.

After Elise put on a beef stew for supper, she peeled the apples and added sugar, cinnamon, and a teaspoon of flour in the bowl with them to bring out the juices. Then she let the mixture set while she made the crust. She'd almost forgotten how nice it was to cook for a man with a good appetite. Cooking for Derrick was very rewarding, and he'd never failed to tell her how much he enjoyed it. She looked forward to serving him a slice of warm apple pie for dessert.

"Oh, that smells delicious, dear," Frieda said as she entered the kitchen a little later, looking somewhat refreshed from her nap. "You made a pie, didn't you?"

"I did. I couldn't resist picking some apples any longer."

"I can't wait to taste it."

"Neither can I," Derrick said as he came in the back door. He crossed the room to kiss his mother on the cheek. "How are you feeling this afternoon?"

"A little better, I believe. I haven't coughed as much today."

"Is that right?" Derrick looked at Elise for confirmation.

"I don't think she has. Hopefully the medicine Dr. Bedslow gave her is beginning to do some good."

"I sure hope so." He sniffed appreciatively. "My kitchen has never smelled as good as it has since you came."

"What did you eat before we got here, son?"

Derrick grinned and shrugged. "Oh, I ate a lot of bacon and eggs—not nearly as good as what you and Elise can make, though." He chuckled. "Oh, and beans—I ate lots of beans. Occasionally neighbors would take pity on me and have me over. They usually sent some leftovers home with me."

Poor man, no wonder he's so complimentary about my cooking, Elise thought as she stirred up some cornmeal, flour, salt, milk, and eggs for corn bread to go with the stew. She checked on her pie to find it golden brown and bubbling. Pulling it out of the oven, she placed it in the pie safe to cool a bit. Then she melted some lard in a skillet, poured the corn bread mixture into it, and slid it into the still-hot oven.

"I'm sorry, son. I should have taught you to cook more than beans and eggs before you left home," Frieda said.

"Mama, I learned a lot from you," Derrick said. "Cooking just isn't something I enjoy doing very much." He turned to leave the kitchen. "I'm going up to clean up before supper. If I stay here, I'll be cutting into that pie before it's cooled enough."

"We'll be near ready to eat when you come back down," Elise said. "It won't take long for the corn bread to finish baking."

"I'll hurry, then."

Elise helped Frieda set out dishes, then ladled the stew into a large soup tureen and brought it to the table. She set it beside Frieda's place so she could serve it. Then Elise brought out the butter and poured Derrick a glass of the cold milk he liked with meals. She put a fresh pot of coffee on so it would be ready to have with the pie. Derrick came back downstairs just as she took the corn bread out of the oven.

No one had to ask Derrick to say the blessing by now, and when he was finished, Frieda ladled the stew into bowls while Elise cut and served the corn bread.

"How are the apples coming along, son?"

"I think we're going to get started with the picking this coming Monday. I'm going into town tomorrow to see about getting someone in to cook for the hands."

"Derrick, there's no need for that. I can cook for them," Elise said. "I've been planning on doing that anyway."

"I don't expect you to do that, Elise. I can hire someone to come do it. There's no need for you to—"

"Helping you at harvest is the least I can do to thank you for your hospitality, Derrick."

"I don't want payment—"

"I wish I was able to do it. I am a little better. Surely I can help," Frieda said, looking from one to the other.

"No!" Elise and Derrick both said at the same time.

"I want you to rest and get your strength back, Mama,"

Derrick continued. "You can protest all you want, but Elise and I know you aren't back to your normal health yet. You must let yourself rest."

"Mama, I know you want to help Derrick out. And you'll have plenty of time for that after you regain your strength. But you aren't up to it for this harvest." Elise turned back to Derrick. "Unless you don't think I can handle it, Derrick, I would like to cook for your harvest. Please."

Derrick looked from his mother to his sister-in-law and shook his head. "You two are a pair. I have no doubt at all that you can handle it, Elise. I accept your offer, and I thank you for it."

"I'll do the best I can. Just let me know what you want me to cook and for how many. I'll do some planning and be ready to go on Monday. Do you serve breakfast and dinner?"

"No, I just provide the midday meal. There will be about twenty people, and they'll work for the whole week—picking first, then packing. We all come back to the yard at noontime. Usually there will be beans or stew or something like that. I think the cook I hired last year made rolls or corn bread. For dessert, there was cake or cobbler, too. But he wasn't the cook you are. I hired him for the week from one of the local ranches. I'll get the supplies for whatever you'd like to make. Just give me a list tomorrow, and I'll go into town."

"Well, you have plenty of apples around. I can make apple cobblers or pies. Fried pies might be good. What do you think, Mama?" Elise asked his mother.

"Why, that's a good idea, Elise. You could make the pies and cobblers up ahead of time, but the fried pies would be easier to serve."

Elise nodded. "That's what I thought. And it's still warm in the middle of the day. . . . Maybe I could make bread this weekend and bake a ham and make sandwiches for them?"

"That would be easy to serve, too," his mother said. "I think both of those are good ideas. What do you think, son?"

Seeing how Elise included his mother in the decision making, even though she couldn't do any of the cooking, made him think even more highly of her. "I think anything you two decide is fine. But the sandwiches and fried pies would sure make it much easier to serve."

"You could even take it all out into the orchard to wherever they're working so they don't have to come back to the house. That would save some time, wouldn't it?" his mother asked.

"It certainly would. I could load up the wagon and take it out to them."

Elise was nodding. "Maybe I could vary the sandwiches between the ham and a roast? I don't think they'd get tired of the fried pies."

"No, I don't either. I'll pick apples for you whenever you're ready for them. I can help peel them, too," Derrick offered.

"I think even I can help do that," his mother said. "See, son, there's no reason to hire anyone. I'm sure your help will be thrilled with whatever Elise comes up with."

"I'll have a list for you in the morning." Elise got up to get a pencil and a piece of paper.

Derrick had a feeling his helpers were going to wish they could work another week after tasting Elise's cooking.

❧

Elise did the wash the next day to get it out of the way, and then on Saturday she made bread while Derrick picked apples. On Sunday afternoon she put a ham in the oven while he and his mother peeled the apples. She cooked them down with cinnamon and sugar, and then after supper that evening she finished making up the individual pies and fried them.

That all started a week that was one of the busiest Elise could ever remember. She was up at sunrise to make breakfast for Derrick, and then she began preparations for dinner. Derrick had sliced the ham for her the night before, and now she only had to lay out the bread and put the sandwiches together. By the time she was through, Frieda had made her way downstairs and helped stack them in a box Derrick had provided. The fried pies were placed in another box. Once he picked up the boxes and took them to the orchard, Elise put a roast on for the next day's meal.

They would have some of it for supper that night, and then she'd make sandwiches out of the rest of the roast the next day. She stirred up another batch of bread and set it to rise. While Frieda took her afternoon nap, Elise made more fried pies, then punched down the bread dough and kneaded it once more. After shaping it and placing it in loaf pans, she set it to rise again. She'd bake the loaves after she took the roast out of the oven.

By the time her head hit the pillow that night, she was totally exhausted. But she was happy that she was able to pay Derrick back for his hospitality—even though he wanted no pay.

She stayed so busy the rest of the week, the days passed in a blur.

❧

Derrick was out in the orchard with his help, working hard, but he had a feeling it was nowhere near as hard as Elise was working. For days she'd been up at dawn and stayed up late making bread, frying pies, or baking cookies, making sure there was plenty of food to go around. And it was excellent. The friends and neighbors who'd come to help him with his harvest went on and on about how good the food was.

She had a way of seasoning everything that made it all taste wonderful. But then, that shouldn't surprise him. Everything she cooked was tasty. She never complained, but by the end of the week, she was looking pretty tired.

"After the freight company picks up my apple crates this afternoon, why don't I take you and Mama into town for supper tonight, Elise? You certainly deserve it," Derrick said when he came to pick up the boxes of food on Friday.

She shook her head. "There's no need. I'm not sure Mama should be out in the night air just yet. I'll just put on a pot of soup to simmer this afternoon. We have bread left."

Derrick could see the exhaustion in her eyes. He had a feeling she would be too tired to go anywhere that evening anyway. "All right, but I do the dishes tonight. And tomorrow we go into town for dinner."

"We'll see how Mama feels tomorrow. As for the dishes, you can dry, but I'll wash."

Her plan sounded even better than his had. "It's a deal."

By the time he came in after seeing his apples off to market, he found his mother, instead of Elise, in the kitchen, setting the table for two.

"What happened? Is Elise all right?"

"She's fine. But I convinced her to take a nap this afternoon and she's still sleeping. She's worked so hard this week. I couldn't bring myself to wake her. The soup she made is done, and there's fresh bread to have with it. I'm still capable of dishing it up, and together we can surely do the dishes."

"I was afraid the week would take a toll on her," Derrick said. He took a couple of bowls from the cupboard and brought them to his mother.

"She handled it all just fine. But it was a busy week, and I think she just relaxed knowing the pace would slow down after today." She ladled the soup into the two bowls and handed them back to Derrick to take to the table. "I'm glad she stepped in, however. After watching her this week, I can admit that I don't think I could have handled it."

"Well, she made a name for herself around here. No one else in the area has ever gotten as many compliments on the food served during harvest week as I did."

"You be sure and tell her."

"I will." He'd wanted to tell her tonight and was disappointed she wasn't here. As wonderful as it was to share supper with his mother, and as happy as he was that she seemed to be getting better, something was missing at the table. And he knew exactly what it was—or rather *who* it was. He missed Elise.

six

Elise woke long before dawn, appalled that she had slept clear thought the night. What must Derrick think of her? She'd left him and Mama to fend for themselves last night! And Mama—was she all right? Elise threw off her covers, dressed quickly, and hurried across the hall to check on her.

Frieda was snoring lightly and seemed to be resting easy. Elise breathed a sigh of relief as she tiptoed out of the room and headed downstairs as quietly as she could. It was still dark outside, but there was a hint of light to the east. Elise lit the stove, put on a pot of coffee, then slipped out the back door to inhale the sweet morning smell and watch the sunrise. She'd come to love it here in New Mexico Territory. She never tired of looking at Derrick's orchard or out at the high mesas and the surrounding farmland dotting the landscape. Even though the view was better from upstairs, Elise found that she could get glimpses of the Animas River from the end of the back porch, and that was where she went now, to wait until the rising sun glinted on its waters.

She really should start thinking about returning to Denver once Frieda was better. But returning to her empty cottage held no appeal for her at all. And she felt sorrowful for that. It was her and Carl's home from the beginning of their marriage, and it held many happy memories. . .but it no longer held him. In fact, if it weren't for the few pictures she had of him, she wasn't sure she could pull his face into her memory. Thoughts of Carl seemed to come farther apart these days.

Maybe it was because she'd been so busy lately. Taking care of Frieda and feeding the workers for Derrick this week had filled her days and nights. There hadn't been much time to think about anything else—or so she told herself. She returned to the kitchen just in time to rescue the coffee before it boiled over. She'd better quit woolgathering and concentrate on what she planned to do today.

She needed to catch up on the wash, but she'd wait until Monday to do that. The apples on the tree out back needed picking for Derrick and Mama's own use. Perhaps she could make some apple jelly and apple butter out of some of them.

Elise took the leftover ham from the icebox and began to slice several pieces off it, saving what was on the bone to put into some pinto beans for supper that evening. She heard Derrick's heavier tread upstairs, alerting her that he would be down soon. Elise began to heat the ham in a frying pan, trying to ignore the fluttery beat of her heart.

❧

Derrick woke from a restless sleep. He'd been out of sorts when he went to bed the night before, and he wasn't in a much better mood when he woke up. Elise had never come downstairs last night, and his mother had retired right after she'd helped him clean up after supper. He'd tried to get her to just sit and talk to him, but Mama wasn't one to let a man do a job she thought belonged to a woman. It didn't seem to matter that he'd been doing all of that before she came.

After she'd gone upstairs, the night had seemed longer than usual in the overly quiet house—even though that's how it had always been before his mother and Elise had arrived. He didn't much like the feel of it now, so he'd headed out to the barn, where he spent the next several hours cleaning equipment and taking care of his animals.

It was the smell of coffee and frying ham drifting up the stairs that finally brightened his mood. Derrick doubted his mother was down yet, so that meant Elise was in the kitchen. Throwing the covers off his bed, he hurried to dress and shave so he could get downstairs and see her.

She looked rested when she turned from the range to greet him. "Good morning, Derrick. I am so sorry I left you and Mama on your own last night. I didn't realize how tired I was, I guess."

Derrick poured himself a cup of coffee. "Well, you were up before dawn and awake until very late at night all week; it's no wonder you couldn't wake up! I can't thank you enough for all you did this week, Elise. You've become quite famous among my neighbors and friends for your tasty sandwiches and fried pies. They couldn't get enough. I think they hated to see the week come to an end."

"I'm glad they liked everything," Elise said, forking the ham slices onto a plate. "We had some leftover ham from the last one I baked. I thought it would be good for breakfast. I'm making biscuits and gravy to go with it."

"You won't hear me complaining," Derrick said.

"Nor me," Frieda said from the kitchen doorway.

"What are you doing here, Mama? You're supposed to—"

"I'm feeling better this morning," his mother said as she took a seat at the table. "Don't worry. I'm not going to start cleaning house or cooking. But I'm just plain tired of staying upstairs, away from everything. If I get weary, I'll take a nap. Otherwise, I can at least peel potatoes or snap beans or fold clothes from right here."

Derrick looked at Elise and grinned. "She's sounding a little grouchy this morning. I think she's on the mend."

"Now what do you mean by that? You'd be grouchy, too, if

you had to stay in your room most of the day."

"Yes, ma'am, I would." Derrick crossed the room and gave his mother a hug before sitting down at the table. "I'm just glad to see you finally feeling a little better."

"So am I, Mama," Elise said, crossing the room to bring his mother a cup of coffee. "I've missed your company."

"Well, I figured I could do a lot just sitting here. And none of it should tax me too much. Derrick, I'm sure you have some things that need mending. If you bring them down, I can work on some of that while I keep Elise company this morning."

"I'd sure like having you down here with me," Elise assured her as she popped a pan of biscuits into the oven and stirred the gravy she'd begun.

"I have a pile of things in need of mending, Mama. I'll go get them after breakfast." He'd sewn on a button here and there, but anything else was beyond what he was willing to tackle. "Just don't feel you have to hurry. They've waited this long. It won't hurt them to wait a little longer."

Derrick wasn't used to having females around from morning to night. At first he wasn't sure how he felt about it, but he was quickly realizing what he'd been missing. The deep loneliness he hadn't realized he'd been living with—until his mother and Elise came—had eased in all kinds of ways. He liked coming in from his orchards knowing someone was there to ask him how his day was going or if he was hungry—knowing there was someone just to talk to.

Elise turned from stirring the gravy. "When do you think we could get the apple tree out back picked? I'd be glad to help—"

"I realized last night I should have done that when I had all that help. I'll do it today. I'm going to be helping Jed with his harvest all next week. I think I can get them all picked today, but if you want to, you could pick some from the lower branches. I don't want you climbing the ladder or up in the tree."

"No," Frieda said and shook her head. "The last thing we need is for you to fall and break something, Elise."

"I'll pick the lower branches, then. I thought I could make some jelly and apple butter for you to have this winter."

"I love apple jelly," Derrick said. "And if I remember right, Mama loves apple butter."

"Mmm, I do."

"Well, there are canning supplies down in the root cellar. I'll get them out and clean them this weekend, too." Elise poured the gravy into a bowl and brought it to the table. Then she took the biscuits out of the oven, plopped them into a napkin-lined basket, and brought them and the ham to the table.

Derrick waited for her to freshen up her cup of coffee and bring it to the table before saying the blessing. "Dear Lord, we thank You for this day. Thank You for letting Mama feel better. Thank You for the outstanding crop of apples this year. Thank You for this wonderful food Elise has prepared for us to eat. Please help us to live this day to Your glory, dear Lord. We thank You most of all for Your precious Son and our Savior and Your plan for our salvation through Him. In Jesus' name I pray. Amen."

He took a bite of gravy and biscuit and sent up a silent addition. *And thank You, Lord, for letting Mama decide to come to Farmington and for bringing Elise with her.*

⁂

Derrick brought down his mending before he headed out to do his morning chores. While Frieda got started on that, Elise cleaned up the kitchen and then went upstairs to make beds and straighten up so that she would be ready to help Derrick pick apples when he was back.

"Is it warm enough for me to sit outside while you two are picking, do you think?" Frieda asked her.

"I think so. I can get your shawl, though, just in case you get cool. The fresh air might do you some good."

"I don't see how it could hurt. I'm feeling kind of cooped up in here."

"Then we'll get you out there for a while," Elise said. "I'll go down to the root cellar later and bring up the canning supplies so I can wash them. I'll just put them in the pantry until I'm ready for them. I figure next week I'll stay busy putting up apples."

"I can peel them for you," Frieda offered as she mended one of Derrick's shirts.

"That will be a great help, Mama." Elise was thrilled that her mother-in-law seemed to be recovering, but she didn't want to tax her. "Just don't feel you have to overdo things."

"I won't."

Derrick opened the back door and peeked inside. "You ready to start picking apples, Elise?"

"I'll be right out. Your mother wants to come out and watch, I think."

Derrick looked over at his mother. "Are you feeling up to that, Mama?"

"Yes, I am."

"All right, I'll bring a chair out for you." He crossed the room to grab a kitchen chair while his mother brought the shirt she'd been working on and followed him outside.

Elise followed them both. Derrick handed her a burlap sack with straps that tied over the shoulder. He helped her put it on and tie it so that the strap rested on the opposite shoulder from the side the bag hung on. "Don't let it get too heavy for you. I have more sacks."

Elise caught her breath at his nearness and could only nod in response.

Derrick put on his own sack and went over to make sure the ladder was secure. "I'm going to start up high. Just be careful to work on the side opposite me so that if I drop an apple, it doesn't fall on you."

It was only after Derrick moved away that Elise seemed to find her voice again. "I'll watch out."

She made her way around the lower branches, picking all she could reach on each one and, after Derrick dropped his first apple, trying to keep clear of the area he was working in.

"Oops, look out, Elise!"

Elise dodged one more falling apple. "I'm not sure there is a safe place to work with you up there, Derrick," Elise teased.

"I'm sorry. I was trying to grab two at a time."

"Trying to show off, huh?"

The teasing banter that ensued between them had Frieda chuckling from the porch.

Elise was nearly through picking from the lower limbs when Derrick yelled, "Elise! Watch out!"

Two more apples fell only a foot away. She could feel the whoosh as they flew by her. Hands on her hips, she looked up to see Derrick peering down at her, concern on his face. "Now what?" she asked laughingly. "Were you trying to grab three this time?"

"I am so sorry. Please—go sit with Mama. You'll be safer there."

"You'd better come on up here," Frieda called. "My son seems to have slippery hands today."

"I think I have most of them. I can pick the rest after you're through."

"I think that would be best," Derrick said with what sounded like relief in his voice. "We've had too many near misses today. I sure don't want you ending up with a concussion."

"No, neither do I."

"I need to come down and get a new sack and move the ladder around. I'll help you get your bag off."

But as Elise turned to move out from under the branches and Derrick started down the ladder, she heard an ominous whoosh as another apple fell. She moved just in time to avoid it hitting her in the head, but the apple struck her upper right arm with surprising force.

"Oh!" She stood rubbing the spot and had a feeling her arm would be bruised soon.

"Elise, did it hit you? I am so sorry. It fell out of the sack—" Derrick broke off midsentence, and the next thing Elise knew, he was standing beside her. He reached out to touch her arm, and she winced.

He quickly pulled his hand away from her arm. "Oh, Elise, I am so very sorry. It's already bruising."

"It wasn't your fault, Derrick. It was an accident."

"I'll go pick some ice off the block and wrap it in cloth to put on Elise's shoulder," Frieda said.

Derrick untied Elise's sack and helped her remove it from her left shoulder. He dropped it to the ground. "I'll bring it in later. Right now, let's just get you comfortable."

"I'm fine, Derrick. It's not broken or anything like that."

"I know it hurts, though." He helped her up to the porch and into the chair his mother had vacated. Frieda came out of the kitchen with a dishcloth-wrapped pack of picked ice. Elise shivered as she put the cold pack on her arm.

"I know it's cold, but it will keep the swelling down," Derrick said.

The pain did begin to ease, and Elise nodded. "It's feeling better. I'm going to be fine. You go on back to work."

Derrick nodded.

Elise insisted Frieda take the chair again, and she sat down on the top step, watching Derrick go back to work. . .until she began to get nervous watching him reach higher than he should and lean out on the ladder farther than she was comfortable with. "I'm going to go in and start dinner."

"I'll come and help," Frieda said.

"No, you stay and watch. It's not going to take long to warm up the soup left from last evening. I'll go ahead and put the beans on for supper, too."

"You sure you're up to it?"

Elise raised her arm so her mother-in-law could see that she could move it. It did hurt, but she grinned to try to hide the grimace that was behind it.

"I'm up to it."

"You're probably going to be even sorer tomorrow," her mother-in-law said with concern in her eyes.

Elise truly hoped not. She made her way to the kitchen and went about heating the soup for dinner.

Soon everything was ready, so she called Frieda and Derrick in to eat. Derrick watched her closely throughout the meal, even though she continued to assure him that she was fine.

"Is there anything I can do before I go back out?" he asked.

"You might bring the canning things up from the root cellar for her," Frieda said. "She wanted to get it all washed."

"I can do that before I finish picking apples," Derrick said.

Elise wasn't going to object. Washing them was one thing; carrying them up from the cellar with her arm still throbbing was another matter. She was glad for the offer. "Thank you. I appreciate it."

"I'll put some of the apples in the pantry and the rest down in the cellar. Will that be all right?"

"That will be fine."

"Don't feel you have to take care of all the apples right away. They stay well in the root cellar," Derrick said.

"I know. I'll do a little at a time. I'll get everything ready and start making jelly next week."

He brought up the canning utensils and empty jars while Elise cleaned up after dinner and got the beans started for supper.

Frieda insisted on drying the dishes and then finally admitted to being tired. "I guess all the excitement of the apple picking wore me out. I think I'll take a nap. Then maybe I can help with supper."

"Don't worry about helping with supper, Mama. You just rest. It was good to have you down here this morning. I'm sorry I gave you such a scare."

"I'm just glad you're all right," Frieda said as she moved toward the stairs.

Derrick brought up the last of the jars and placed them in the kitchen for Elise to wash. "Did Mama finally decide to take a rest?"

"Yes. I think watching you swing from the tree and seeing me get hurt was too much for her."

Derrick looked into Elise's eyes. "Seeing you get injured was almost too much for me. How is your arm? It looks really bad."

Elise looked down and could see that the bruise on her arm was turning blue-black. "It looks worse than it feels."

"I doubt that, but I have a feeling you aren't going to tell me how bad it really hurts." He reached up and tucked an escaping tendril of hair behind her ear. "I really am sorry, Elise. Please call me if you need to lift anything heavy or if you need anything at all."

His nearness had her breath catching in her throat once more. All she could manage was a nod as she turned to the sink and began to wash pots, jars, and lids.

seven

Derrick went back to picking apples feeling torn. He wanted to stay in the kitchen and help Elise. Much as she tried to hide it, he could tell that her arm was hurting her. He was glad she'd gotten a good night's sleep last night, because he had a feeling she wouldn't be sleeping well at all tonight. He was sure that arm was going to be hurting even worse the next day.

That Elise had worked to the point of exhaustion just to help him out this week and then got hurt helping him pick apples was very eye-opening for Derrick. He'd been attracted to her long ago when she only held the promise of the woman she had become. She was a special lady, and he was realizing that what he'd thought he felt for her years ago was nothing compared to what he was beginning to feel for her now.

Elise pitched in wherever needed. She'd come through with the cooking for all the hands, and she'd been waiting on his mother for the past few weeks. The house was always neat and tidy. Clothes were always clean and pressed. And she never complained.

It'd become pure joy to have this pretty, joyful woman, whom he'd cared about for years, in his house—making it a home. The house had never smelled as good as it did from the mouth-watering aromas of fresh bread, roasted chicken, or beef stew—and especially those apple pies Elise made. He'd always gotten by on his own cooking, but he fully appreciated the difference now.

Derrick sighed as he plucked two more apples off the tree

and put them in his sack. Life as he knew it had changed—and he didn't want to go back to the way it had been. With his mother and Elise here, loneliness was a thing of the past. He was very happy to have his mother here—he'd missed being around family very much—but it was Elise who had him sprucing up first thing in the morning and before supper at night. It was she who had his heart thudding when she smiled at him each morning, and his pulse taking off at a gallop when his fingers had grazed her cheek as he'd tucked that tendril of hair behind her ear earlier. It was Elise who had him cringing at the bruise from the apple and wishing he could hurt for her.

He wasn't sure what to do about the attraction he felt for her. He didn't know whether to pursue her or not. She was a widow and free to marry again. But she was his *brother's* widow, and she'd obviously loved Carl. Derrick wasn't sure that he could compete with his brother's memory, and for the sake of family relationships, he didn't know if he should even try. His mother and Elise were close, and he knew they loved each other. If his desire to court Elise became evident and made her feel uncomfortable being in his home, he wasn't sure what it might do to her and his mother's relationship. He didn't want to harm it. Elise was the daughter his mother had never had.

She was in his thoughts more often than not, and while he fought to force his thinking on other things, he just didn't know how to keep her out of his dreams at night. She'd been a frequent visitor to them for a very long time—and he had a feeling she always would be.

❧

While Derrick finished picking apples and Frieda was napping, Elise made another packet of ice with a dish towel and wrapped it around her throbbing arm just long enough to ease the pain for a bit. After she washed the rest of the canning utensils, she peeled and sliced potatoes. She'd just put them on to fry when Derrick brought in a sack of apples.

"I'll put these in the pantry so you can get to them easily. The rest I'll put in the root cellar until you want them. Just let me know, and I'll bring up what you need."

"Thank you, Derrick."

It didn't take long before he had all the apples brought in and stored away. He came back into the kitchen and asked, "How is your arm feeling?"

Elise was glad she could answer honestly, since she'd used the ice packet, "It's better."

"I'm glad. I'll go feed the horses and check on the rest of the animals and then come help you with supper."

Elise wasn't used to a man helping in the kitchen. "You don't have to do that."

"I know. But it was my fault you got hurt today. Helping with supper is the least I can do for you, Elise." Derrick paused for a moment, his gaze meeting hers from across the room.

There was something about the look in his eyes that had Elise's heart beating against her ribs as she waited for him to continue.

"My brother was a very lucky man to have you as his wife." With that said, Derrick turned and headed back outside.

It was a good thing he left just then, because Elise couldn't find her voice and didn't know what to say if she could have. She felt as if the breath had been knocked plumb out of her, and it was all she could do not to read anything into his words. Just because she was attracted to him didn't mean. . . Or did it?

"Elise," Frieda said, coming in from her nap, "I'm sorry I slept so long."

Elise blew out a deep breath and turned to her mother-in-law. "Don't worry about it, Mama. You were up longer than usual today."

"What do you need me to do?"

Help me to stop daydreaming about Derrick, was on the tip of her tongue, but Elise caught herself just before the words left her lips. She pulled her attention to the question Frieda had asked her and thought for a moment. The beans were about done; the potatoes were frying. "You can cut up some onion for me to put in the potatoes."

While Frieda chopped the onion, Elise mixed up a pan of corn bread to go with the beans and popped it into the oven. Then she checked the potatoes; they were brown and crisp on the bottom, so she carefully turned them over, adding the onions Frieda had cut up. This was one of their favorite meals, and she hoped Derrick liked it, too.

Frieda was just finishing setting the table when Derrick came back inside. "Oh, that smells wonderful, Elise. Is there anything you need me to do?"

"No. It's all about ready," Elise said, trying to ignore the way her pulse raced when he entered the room. She couldn't help but notice that he'd washed up outside before coming inside. "We're just waiting for the corn bread and the potatoes to finish cooking."

He crossed the room to kiss his mother on the cheek. "And how are you feeling, Mama? Did you have a good nap?"

"Yes, I slept hard. Must have been that fresh air outside—or the stress from watching Elise get hurt and you weaving all over those tree limbs to pick the apples."

Derrick chuckled. "Hopefully it was just the fresh air."

Elise slipped a tray of fried pies, left from the day before, onto the back of the range to heat up while they ate. She began to ladle the beans into individual bowls.

"I can at least take these to the table," Derrick said.

"Yes, you can do that." Elise smiled at him. It was nice that he wanted to help. While he took the bowls and set them in the middle of the dinner plates Frieda had set the table with, Elise pulled the corn bread out of the oven and set it to the side. She dished up the potatoes into a large bowl and handed it to Derrick to take to the table.

She cut the corn bread into slices, but before she could lift the pan, Derrick had grabbed it. "That's too heavy with your arm hurting. I'll take it to the table."

Elise followed with the butter and then started back to get the water pitcher.

"I'll get that. Please, Elise, just go sit down," Derrick said.

Carl was a good husband, but he hadn't been one to help in the house much. Elise wasn't quite sure what to make of the fact that Derrick was a more-than-willing helper.

Once everything was on the table, Derrick bowed his head. "Dear Father, thank You for our many blessings. Thank You that Elise wasn't hurt any worse than she was today. Please let her arm heal quickly, and please let Mama continue to regain her strength. Thank You for this food we are about to eat. In Jesus' name I pray. Amen."

Frieda served the potatoes and corn bread, and after a few bites, Derrick was lavish in his compliments on the meal.

Suppertime was quickly becoming one of Elise's favorite times of the day.

❧

Elise's arm did hurt more the next day, but she tried not to let on as she went about making breakfast so that they could get to church on time. Going to church on Sunday was Frieda's only outing of the week, and while it did tire her, Elise knew there was no way she was going to miss church. The members had made them feel very welcome, and Elise would have hated to miss going, too.

The preacher's wife, Rachel, had made a special effort to talk to them and introduce them to others of the church family. Today she came up to them as soon as they sat down. "How are you settling in, Mrs. Morgan?"

"It's beginning to feel like home, and I like it here a lot." Frieda smiled at the younger woman. "But I'll feel more at home if you call me Frieda instead of Mrs. Morgan."

"Frieda it is, then. I'm glad you're settling in." Rachel turned to Elise. "And how do you like Farmington, Elise?"

"I like it—what I have seen of it. I certainly love the countryside."

"Are you thinking of staying, then?"

"Oh, I'll need to get back to Denver before too long. It's where my home is," Elise said. And then she wondered how her house was going to feel like home when she was settling in here so easily. And how empty was the house going to feel when the others who'd made it home for her were no longer there? She pushed those thoughts to the back of her mind. She didn't want to think about going home yet. Frieda still needed her, and as long as that was the case, she didn't have to think about returning to Colorado.

"Well, I'm sure you could sell your home up there and relocate down here in New Mexico Territory."

Elise wasn't sure how to reply, and she was relieved when Rachel hurried off to speak to someone else who'd just arrived. Elise couldn't help but admit to herself that Rachel's idea was one she'd thought of herself. But she couldn't live with Mama and Derrick forever. It was one thing while she was needed; it would be something else entirely to just expect to stay. She put her attention on the church service, where it should be, instead of weaving daydreams on what-ifs and maybes.

Harold Burton's sermon was a good reminder about putting one's trust in the Lord and looking to Him for guidance. Elise wasn't sure she always gave things over to Him, but she was going to strive to do so from now on. When the service was over, she stood with a renewed determination to let the Lord lead her as she followed Derrick and Frieda down the aisle.

"Let's go over to the Grand Hotel for Sunday dinner," Derrick suggested as they left the church after telling Harold what a good sermon he'd given.

"I can make something at home, Derrick."

"I know you can. But that arm is bound to be bothering you today. And besides, I think Mama would like to enjoy her outing a little longer."

"I wouldn't mind," Frieda agreed, "especially as it's such a nice day."

"I'll drive you both around to see some of the area after we eat," Derrick said.

Elise wasn't going to turn down the offer. Frieda had commented on feeling all cooped up lately, and she wouldn't mind seeing more of the countryside herself.

Elise enjoyed the meal at the hotel very much. The dining room was nicely decorated, and on Sundays they served everything family style.

"This is good," Derrick said after taking his first bite of fried chicken. "But it doesn't hold a candle to yours, Elise."

"Why, thank you, Derrick. I was thinking it was better than mine."

"No, it's not," Frieda assured her, "but I know how you feel. Sometimes it's just good to eat someone else's cooking."

Elise guessed she was right, because everything tasted great to her.

After dinner, Derrick showed them around the town, passing the drugstore where they'd taken Frieda's prescription to be filled and the newspaper office and one of the cafés.

"What is that, son?" Frieda asked as they passed an adobe building.

"It's an Indian trading post, Mama."

"Oh? Is that like a general store or mercantile?"

"I guess you could consider it that way. You can find warm blankets there, and pottery and baskets, among other things. They make wonderful fry bread."

"There are a lot of Indians in this area?" Elise asked.

"Yes. There are Navajo, Jicarilla Apache, and Ute tribes in this area. They were here long before Farmington became the town it is now."

From there, Derrick took them out to see some of his neighbors' orchards and farms. "The soil in this area is very rich, and with the Animas, San Juan, and La Plata rivers all converging, it makes it easy to grow just about anything."

Elise could see how it was likely to become a major farming community in the years to come. Derrick had been very smart to settle here.

By the time they arrived back home, she knew she could be happy living in this area for the rest of her life. But it wasn't likely that was going to happen. She really needed to try to look forward to returning to Colorado, but Elise had a feeling that was going to be very hard to do.

≈

The next morning, it was Derrick's turn to help a neighbor

with his harvest, and Elise got up earlier than usual to make breakfast for him before he left. His smile, when he entered the kitchen and found her at the stove, made it worth the effort.

"I thought I must be imagining that smell of bacon frying. You didn't have to do this, Elise. I would have grabbed a couple of cold biscuits and eaten them on the way over to Jed's."

"That's not a good way to start the day," she said as she dished up the bacon onto a plate. She cracked three eggs into the skillet and cooked them over-easy for him. "And don't worry about milking Bessie. I'll do it after you leave."

"Elise, I can't let you do that," Derrick said as he poured himself a cup of coffee.

"Derrick, I know how to milk a cow. I grew up on a farm just like you did."

"I know, but—"

"I'm sure Jed needs you over there as soon as possible. You were glad for those who showed up early here." She took a pan of biscuits out of the oven.

"I was."

"Well then, I can milk Bessie and gather the eggs and feed the chickens while you're helping others out."

"Elise, your arm—"

"Feels better today." Elise handed him a plate filled with bacon and eggs and biscuits. "It looks worse than it feels."

She fixed her own plate and brought it to the table. She bowed her head while Derrick said the blessing, and then she looked up to find his gaze on her.

He shook his head. "You are some woman, Elise. I'm not going to let you milk Bessie. I'll do that. But you can gather the eggs and feed the chickens, if you will."

From the look in his eyes, Elise had a feeling there would be no sense in arguing with him. She nodded. "All right."

≈

The end of September and first part of October seemed to fly by as they settled into a routine of sorts. Derrick milked Bessie while Elise made his breakfast. After he left to help with other harvests, she fed the chickens and brought in the eggs. Then when Frieda came down, she made breakfast for her.

She stayed busy during the day—making apple butter and jelly, doing the washing and the ironing. She baked bread and churned butter, cleaned house and helped Frieda with the mending. And she looked forward to the minute Derrick would walk in the back door and sniff appreciatively of anything she had cooking.

Frieda was better but still not up to taking care of Derrick and his home by herself. For the time being, Elise was happy to push thoughts of returning to Denver to the back of her mind.

But as the days went by, Elise found that her thoughts of Carl had all but disappeared. The fact that she could no longer readily recall his sweet face brought her deep guilt. Instead, and hard as she tried to avoid it, she found herself thinking of Derrick more and more each day. Was it because he was the only man she'd been around for any length of time since Carl's death? She sighed and shook her head. She didn't know. All she did know was that Derrick wasn't only in her thoughts during the day; he'd come to occupy her dreams at night, and was the first person she thought about when she woke.

His smile, when he came into the kitchen after milking the cow each morning and found her dishing up his breakfast, had her heart doing little somersaults. She never tired of the compliments he showered on her over her cooking or of his appreciation for all she did for him and his mother.

It was while she sat under the apple tree out back, taking a break one afternoon, that she realized she could no longer deny that her feelings for Derrick were growing with each passing day. But she had no business feeling this way about her husband's brother. While the very thought of leaving here broke her heart. . .maybe it was time to make plans to return to Denver.

❧

Derrick found himself looking forward to coming home each evening. It was getting dark by the time he returned, and his house was lit with light. He always felt welcomed into his own home as he walked into the kitchen to find Elise cooking supper and his mother setting the table. Life was good.

Tonight he fed his horse and washed up before going inside. But as he started to open the back door and enter the kitchen, he heard his mother exclaim, "No, Elise, you can't go home now! Why, I need you and Derrick needs you."

Derrick felt as if the breath had been knocked right out of him as he waited to hear what Elise had to say.

"Mama, don't worry. I won't leave until you've recovered. But it's something I need to be thinking about once you're well. I've already been gone a long time."

It was only when Derrick heard Elise say she wasn't leaving just yet that he realized he'd been holding his breath. He let it out with a whoosh, not sure whether to be relieved that she was staying for the time being or devastated that she was planning to leave at some time in the future. His heart grew heavy in his chest at the thought of her going back to Denver.

He loved Elise—had always loved her. And he was falling more in love with her with each passing day. All he could think to do was pray.

Dear Lord, please don't let me lose Elise again.

eight

"What's this? You're thinking of leaving us? Are we working you too hard, Elise?"

Elise turned swiftly to find that Derrick had entered the kitchen. His brow was furrowed as he waited for her answer. She rubbed her suddenly pounding temple. She hadn't meant to cause such a stir. "Of course you aren't working me too hard, Derrick. And I wouldn't think of leaving until Mama is fully recovered."

"What's this all about, then? Are you homesick?"

Elise knew him well enough by now to know that the expression in his eyes was one of concern. But she couldn't tell him that the very last thing she wanted to do was return to Denver. Or that she was fast losing her heart to him—or that she felt guilty that she was having trouble remembering what his brother looked like without the aid of a picture. But she wasn't homesick, so she could answer his second question truthfully. "No, I'm not homesick."

"Elise, have I done anything to make you feel unwelcome?"

"No, of course you haven't! You've made me feel right at home." *Too much so*, she thought. But she couldn't say that, either.

"Is there anything you need to go back to Denver to take care of?"

Grasping at anything she could answer truthfully, she said, "Eventually I'll need to check on my home, Derrick. I wasn't planning on staying for an extended period when I left."

"Is there a neighbor you could send a letter or telegram to asking him or her to check on things for you?"

"Mrs. Nordstrom knows where you are, Elise," Frieda said. "You could send her a key and ask her to check on things."

Elise wasn't really worried about the house, but she grasped at any excuse to get out of the conversation. "I could do that. I could send her your key. I probably should have contacted her before now. That's a good idea, Mama. I'll write her tonight."

"Good. Then you can stop worrying about things in Colorado," her mother-in-law said.

"I have to pass the post office on my way to Ed Holly's place tomorrow. I'll be glad to send it off for you."

"Thank you, Derrick." Elise was more confused than ever. She was both relieved and apprehensive—relieved that she didn't have to go home just yet and apprehensive because she knew that staying longer would more than likely make it heart wrenching for her when she did return to Denver. She already felt sick inside at the very thought of leaving.

During supper, no more mention was made about her going back to Colorado. But as she finished cleaning up the kitchen after the meal, Elise turned to find Derrick bringing in a box containing Frieda's writing supplies.

"Mama asked me to bring these to you. She said you might need them to write to your neighbor."

"She's right. I didn't bring letter-writing materials with me. Thank you, Derrick."

"It's no problem." He put the things down on the kitchen table. "I'm glad to do it for you. If I haven't said so lately, I'm very thankful that you came with Mama and have been willing to stay. I know you do have a life in Denver and we've taken up a lot of your—"

"Derrick, I'm not in that big of a hurry to go home. I just

was mentioning to Mama that I probably needed to think about returning. She does seem to be getting better, and even though I know she's not fully back to normal yet, I'm sure you didn't think I would be here this long when you asked me to stay until she was better."

"Neither of us did. But, Elise, even if Mama was completely well, I want you to know that you are always welcome here. . . for as long as you want to stay. You are part of this family, and you always will be."

"Thank you, Derrick." Elise felt a sudden urge to cry at his sweet words and turned to hang up the dish towel with which she'd just dried the last dish. Derrick was a wonderful man, and knowing she would always be welcome in his home meant a great deal to her. But she couldn't keep from wondering if he'd still be so hospitable to her if he knew how much she'd come to care for him. Not as Carl's brother—but as the man who could make her heart turn to mush with just the hint of his smile or the sound of his laughter.

૨૪

Derrick wasn't sure what to say next. Hearing Elise talk about going back to Denver had thrown him into a panic, and all he'd wanted to do was take her in his arms and tell her that he never wanted her to leave his home. And it was what he still wanted to do.

But he was afraid that action might send her running right out the door. She was his brother's widow, and Derrick had no reason at all to believe that she felt the same way—or ever would. To her, he was probably just Carl's brother and Frieda's younger son.

Elise wasn't aware that he'd cared about her for a very long time, and he had no idea how to—or even if he should—let her know how he felt about her. He certainly didn't want to say or do anything that would have her catching the next stage out of town.

"Would you like a cup of coffee?" Elise asked, easing the uncomfortable moment for him. "There's some apple pie left, if you'd like some of that."

"Thank you, I would. But I can get it. You go ahead and write your letter." He would feel much better once she sent that letter off to her neighbor. Maybe then she wouldn't worry about getting back to her house.

She sat down at the table and pulled the ink jar and writing paper toward her. Derrick poured himself a cup of coffee and cut a piece of pie from the one sitting in the pie safe, listening to the scratch of pen against paper. He breathed a sigh of relief that she was writing the letter. He sat down at the table across from her to eat his pie while she finished her correspondence.

It didn't take long before she put the pen down and reread the letter. She nodded, seeming to be satisfied. "Now I just need to get the key from Mama."

"Oh, she gave it to me as she was going upstairs." He stood and dug into his pocket, pulling out Frieda's key to the house in Denver.

"That's all I need." Elise took the key from him and sighed. "Surely I can trust Mrs. Nordstrom with it. I've known her for many years."

"I'm sure you can, Elise. Mama is a good judge of character. She wouldn't have suggested her if she didn't think your neighbor could be trusted."

"That's true. And they were pretty good friends even though Mrs. Nordstrom is younger than Mama." Elise slipped the key into the envelope with the letter and sealed it with Frieda's wax. Then she handed the envelope to Derrick.

"I'll be sure to get it mailed tomorrow." He certainly hoped that would settle her mind about the house and that there'd be no more talk about leaving. Not for a long time.

❧

Before Elise knew it, Thanksgiving was almost upon them. October had passed swiftly with Derrick helping his neighbors and friends. Harvest was over now, and she thought Derrick's workload would slow down, but he kept very busy. He planted more apple trees of varying kinds and took care of all sorts of things in the barn—cleaning it and the other outbuildings, fixing broken equipment, and getting everything in good working order. He took care of the livestock and tried to do all the things he didn't have time for during growing season.

The weather had changed quickly, with the mornings and evenings turning much colder. Derrick always had the stove lit and a fire in the fireplace by the time Elise came down in the morning. He kept wood chopped and stacked out by the back door, but he always made sure there was plenty of wood right inside so that Elise didn't have to bring it in.

Derrick was the most considerate man she'd ever known—even more so than his brother had been. He brought up potatoes and apples from the root cellar to the pantry so they would be easy for Elise to get to. He put up a lean-to over the wash kettle to keep the wind from making it colder than usual to do the wash.

Because he was right there, Derrick was in and out a lot during the day. Elise didn't mind at all—except for the fact that it was becoming very difficult for her to hide her growing feelings for him. She could feel the telltale color creep up her neck each time Derrick popped into the kitchen to see what was cooking or when he complimented her on the meal he'd just eaten.

She could tell when he walked up behind her just from the tickly feeling along the back of her neck. He was very thoughtful. He always seemed to know when she needed help hanging clothes on the line, and before they went to church on Sunday, he'd warm several large stones and put them in the wagon for his mother and Elise to prop their feet on.

Going to church was still Frieda's biggest outing, and she enjoyed it immensely. The people of the church they attended had gone out of their way to make them all feel at home. They'd been asked to join several different families for Sunday dinner during the last month, and Frieda was happily getting to know their neighbors. Several of the ladies had come out to have afternoon tea with them. The days seemed to speed by.

This afternoon was no different. Elise found herself on the back porch, sipping her coffee and looking down toward the river, easier to see now that the leaves were gone from the trees. The river sparkled in the sunlight, and the winter landscape was as beautiful, in its own way, as it had been in late summer. She was sure it would be beautiful in the spring with all the apple trees in bloom. But now she was looking forward to the first snow.

Farmington was a place where she could be happy living for the rest of her life. In fact, she never wanted to leave. But that presented a problem in itself. She didn't know how she could stay—falling in love with Derrick as she was.

She closed her eyes and sent up a silent prayer. *Dear Lord, I don't know what to do. Should I stay or go? Mama seems a little better, but she's not up to keeping house for Derrick or cooking three meals a day. I know he would help her, but I want to be the one cooking for the two of them. I want to be the one taking care of the house. I don't want to go back to Denver. There's nothing there for me to go home to. Lord, please help me to know what to do. I'm afraid if I stay too much longer, it will be even harder to leave. And yet the last thing I want to do is go now—or ever. Please help me, Father. Show me what You would have me do. In Jesus' name I pray. Amen.*

❧

"Elise! Are you out back?" Derrick called out the kitchen door. It wasn't like her not to be in the kitchen this time of day.

"I'm out here, Derrick." Elise hurried around the corner of the porch. "I've been enjoying the crisp air this afternoon. What's wrong?"

He opened the door wide as she came inside. "Nothing is wrong. I just wanted to ask you something and I didn't know where you were."

"Did you need something?"

He looked at her for a moment without saying anything. How did he tell her that he needed to know where she was at all times, that he loved seeing her at the stove, in his house, doing anything around there? He just needed to see *her*. "Not really. I just. . . Do you need anything from town for the Thanksgiving meal? I thought I would go in tomorrow or the next day."

"Oh. It's nearly upon us, isn't it?"

"It is. And I was wondering. . ." He paused.

"What?" she prodded.

Derrick sighed. He didn't think she'd mind, but he wouldn't know for sure until he asked. "For the past several years, I've gone to Jed Barrister's for Thanksgiving. He and his wife Caroline have had me over to their house for dinner. But she's expecting a baby anytime now, and Jed's mentioned a time or two that she tires real easy. I thought maybe—"

"Oh yes, of course. You'd like to have them over here?" She smiled and tilted her head to the side as she waited for his answer.

"Yes, if it's all right with you. Mama said it was fine with her."

"I think that would be wonderful! With just the three of us, there will be way too much to eat anyway, if I make everything Mama says you'd like."

Derrick chuckled. "Mama is just trying to make up for all those Thanksgivings we were apart."

"Well, I think it's very nice that you want to invite Jed and Caroline over. Please do. I know Mama will love having company."

"You're sure? I'll help in any way you need me to."

"I'm sure. I'll start a list of things we need tonight."

"Thank you, Elise."

"You're welcome. But you really didn't need to ask me. This is *your* home, Derrick."

He shook his head. "You're the one who will be doing all the work."

"Oh, don't worry. I'll be putting you to work, too."

"Good." He could think of nothing better than working alongside Elise.

Over the next few days, they did just that. Jed and Caroline eagerly accepted his invitation to Thanksgiving dinner, and Derrick didn't know who seemed more excited about it—them or his mother and Elise. He had to admit that he was looking forward to having company over, too. He knew his home would be gleaming from top to bottom from the cleaning Elise had started that morning. It would be nice to welcome his friends into what had become a warm and hospitable home.

Elise and his mother had gone over their list one last time before he headed off to town for supplies, and when he returned that afternoon, he found them both in the kitchen. Mama was polishing the silverware that'd been stored in the dining room, and Elise was washing the china he'd bought with the house. He put up the supplies in the pantry and came back to help.

"My, I didn't realize I owned such beautiful things," Derrick said, picking up a plate and drying it.

"I still can't believe you bought this house completely furnished, son. We're going to set a beautiful table in that dining room we've never eaten in."

"We can eat right here in the kitchen, Mama. You two don't need to go to all this trouble."

"Oh, don't say that, Derrick. Mama has wanted to eat in there ever since we got here."

"If you can't eat in there for Thanksgiving, then what's the purpose of having a room like that?" his mother asked.

"If you two wanted to eat in there, then why haven't we?"

His mother and Elise looked at each other and shrugged. Elise grinned and shook her head. "The table just seemed kind of big for the three of us for everyday use. And we didn't want you to think we were putting on airs."

Derrick laughed. He couldn't imagine his mother or Elise "putting on airs." "How about if we start out slow. We can use it for holidays, and if you two want to, we could eat Sunday dinners in there, too."

"Well, I think we should," his mother said. "It's a shame not to use a room like that."

"Good. It's settled, then. Sunday dinners and holidays we'll eat in the dining room." They both looked so pleased. Derrick wished he'd known how much they wanted to eat in the formal room. He'd have suggested it long ago.

The next two days were full of activity. While he shelled pecans, Mama chopped them up. Then Elise baked pecan and pumpkin pies and a three-layer chocolate cake thickly iced with chocolate frosting and decorated with pecans.

On the day before Thanksgiving, Elise made corn bread for dressing and put Derrick to work chopping onions and celery. His mother set the table in the dining room with the linens she'd found in the large sideboard.

On Thanksgiving morning, Derrick got up and went to light the stove only to find that Elise was already bustling around the kitchen, humming to herself. She'd lit the oven herself and put the turkey in to roast.

"I should have known you'd be up with the chickens this morning," he said.

"I was too excited to sleep," Elise replied, pouring him a cup of coffee and handing it to him.

"You really enjoy all this cooking, don't you?"

"I do. I'm looking forward to the day."

He was, too. It was the first Thanksgiving he'd enjoyed thinking about in years. He just wished he could tell her that she was the one who was making it so very special for him.

When Jed and Caroline arrived, Elise joined him in welcoming them into his home, and his mother took the young woman under her wing, giving her a baby bonnet she'd managed to crochet in the last few days. Caroline seemed to thrive with the attention his mother and Elise gave her, and Jed beamed seeing his wife enjoy herself so much.

After everyone was seated around the table in the dining room, and before they began to eat the delicious meal Elise had prepared, Derrick bowed his head and prayed. "Dear Lord, we thank You for this day and for all of the many blessings You've bestowed on us. We thank You for friends and family to share this day with, and we thank You for this wonderful meal we are about to eat. Most of all, we thank You for Your Son and our Savior, Jesus Christ. It is in His name we pray. Amen."

Derrick couldn't remember when he'd enjoyed a day more. His house had become a real home thanks to his mother and Elise, and he was happy he'd been able to ask Jed and Caroline over.

That evening, after the Barristers had gone home, he helped his mother and Elise with the cleanup. As they talked over the day, Derrick knew his joy had been complete because he had the two women he loved the most here to share it with. It was a day he would never forget—and one he prayed would not be the last of its kind.

nine

Thanksgiving had been a blessing for Elise. . .if for no other reason than it seemed to have perked Frieda up considerably. The last few Thanksgivings, after Carl passed away, had been very hard on both of them. But this one was different and special because they were able to share it with Derrick, who hadn't been around family in so long. It did her heart good to see him so happy.

Frieda seemed to have regained some of her energy and began helping Elise in the kitchen a little more often. Elise watched and learned as her mother-in-law made her chicken fricassee—one of Derrick's favorite dishes. Carl hadn't liked it much, so there had been no reason for Elise to learn to make it before now. But after seeing Derrick's expression when he took his first bite of the dish, Elise was determined to learn what some of his other favorites were.

"I think you must like chicken better than Carl did. He preferred beef."

"I like beef, too," Derrick said. "But there aren't many ways you can cook a chicken that I don't like."

"Carl was just a little pickier than Derrick," Frieda said. "But they both ate what was put before them. Derrick just enjoyed more of it than Carl did."

"And so Mama began to make more of what Carl liked."

"Son, I didn't play favorites. You know that."

Derrick chuckled. "I do. I'm just teasing you."

Elise couldn't help but wonder if he'd been right, though.

It probably had been easier to make what Carl wanted since Derrick liked it all.

That night, after she'd cleaned the kitchen, Elise looked through the *Fannie Farmer Cookbook* that Frieda had brought with her. There were several chicken dishes she thought she might try. She flipped the pages looking for more.

Derrick came in a little later. "Would you like some cocoa? Mama said she would, and I have a hankering for it, too."

"That sounds good." Elise shut the cookbook. "I'll—"

"No, you sit. I know how to make it. It's one thing I make really well."

"I'd love a cup, then," Elise said, watching him gather the cocoa, sugar, and milk. He pulled out a battered old pan she rarely used and put it on top of the range.

"Mama taught me how long ago. I love it this time of year—makes me sleep better."

Frieda came into the kitchen with her crochet bag. She'd found something to keep her hands busy in quiet moments. She loved to crochet, and after meeting Caroline, she was busily crocheting a complete layette for the baby-to-come. Her hands seemed to be flying across the piece she was working on as Derrick went about making the cocoa.

He moved the teakettle over so that the water would boil, and he put milk in the pan to scald it. Elise watched him mix the cocoa and sugar. He added a pinch of salt and mixed it in. Elise thought he added something else, but she couldn't see what it was. Once he decided that the milk was ready, he poured boiling water into the dry mixture and stirred it into a paste. Then he added it all to the milk and stirred it again, bringing it to a near boil.

The kitchen smelled delicious. Elise felt as though she should be helping, but it was Derrick's kitchen after all, and he seemed to want to do this for them. He filled three cups with the aromatic liquid, then brought Elise and his mother a cup. Then he brought his own over and joined them at the table.

Elise lifted the cup to her mouth and blew on it. "Mmm. It smells wonderful, Derrick." She took a small sip. "This is delicious."

"Thank you."

"I think it's better than mine," his mother said. "What did you add to it, Derrick?"

"Just a hint of cinnamon."

"Ah." Elise nodded. "That's what it is. It's very good."

"Thank you. I'm glad I can make something for the two of you."

It quickly became a family custom for Derrick to make them cocoa before bedtime. It was a time of day Elise found herself looking forward to. Frieda and Derrick shared memories that she'd never heard before, and with each passing day she felt she knew Derrick better.

≥∂

By the first week of December, Derrick's mother was making great progress with the layette. She began on the tiny booties one evening while Elise was finishing up another batch of jelly and Derrick was reading the newspaper. He loved this time of day with them. He would read them tidbits from the paper from time to time. Even if there wasn't much talking going on, there was always a cozy feeling in his kitchen that he couldn't seem to get enough of.

"Derrick, I so enjoyed having the Barristers over for Thanksgiving," his mother said as she crocheted. "It made me think of the family custom we used to have—up until you and Carl became adults. Then your papa and I continued it on a smaller scale. Do you remember what it was?"

"Of course I do. I don't think a Christmas goes by that I don't think about it. We used to take candy and baked goods to neighbors and friends the day before Christmas Eve."

"I truly enjoyed doing that at Christmastime."

"Well, Mama, I have to admit it's not a family custom I've kept up. Before you and Elise got here, I was doing good just to cook for myself."

Frieda chuckled. "Son, I sure didn't expect you to keep up with it. Elise and I did it on a smaller scale in Denver. We usually made cookies for the neighbors on each side of us. But that was about it."

"I remember that Carl and I always went with you and Papa to deliver everything when we were young. And you bade us to mind our manners."

"Which you always did. You were both good boys." She sighed and looked thoughtful. "It would be nice to start the tradition back up here. I don't want to put it all onto Elise, but I think I'm feeling up to making some candy and cookies. What do you two think? Could we do it?"

Derrick exchanged a glance with Elise. He hadn't heard his mother sound so enthused about anything in a long time. But even though she seemed to be doing better, he knew most of the work would fall to Elise.

"I don't see why not," Elise said.

"I can help shell pecans and chop them. . .and whatever else you need me to do," he hurried to assure her. No wonder he was falling in love with Elise. She was perfectly aware that she'd be doing most of the work, but because his mother wanted to do it, she readily agreed.

"Well, we need to do first things first. Derrick, you need to make us a list of your neighbors and friends—anyone you'd like to give to. Just make sure you include them all. We don't want to have any of them feeling slighted. Then we can figure out what to make and how much of it."

It was wonderful, if a bit surprising, to see his mother take control of the planning, and he and Elise were quick to agree with her. "I'll start making a list tonight, Mama," Derrick said.

"I'll check the pantry to see what we have on hand after I clean up here," Elise said as she put the lid on the last jar of jelly.

"You two don't have to do it all tonight." Frieda paused in crocheting another round of tiny stitches. "Tomorrow will be soon enough."

"You know, we could ask Harold about the needy around here that I don't know personally," Derrick said. "I'm sure there are some people around here who could really use a helping hand this Christmas. I've been very blessed with a bumper crop of apples. I'd like to do something to help the less fortunate."

"That's a wonderful suggestion, Derrick." Elise took several jars of apple jelly to the pantry.

"Yes, it is. I like that idea a lot, son," his mother said. "Please do check with Preacher Burton."

Derrick got up to begin making cocoa. "I will. I'll go into town tomorrow and ask him about it."

"We could make a list of the things you enjoyed giving out, if you'd like, Mama," Elise said as she came out of the pantry.

"All right. I think I can remember most of it."

"I'll get some paper so I can write it down. Then after Derrick finds out how many people we're talking about, we can decide what might work best."

Elise got the paper and a pencil and sat back down just as Derrick served their cocoa. Elise took a sip before asking,

"What were your favorite things to give out?"

"Everyone liked my sugar cookies. And I took gingerbread. I made fudge and fondant, too. What were your favorites, Derrick?"

He brought his cup to the table and sat down. "I thought we made up some popcorn balls some years."

"We did," his mother said, nodding. "What else?"

"You made molasses cookies, didn't you?"

"Yes, I did! They were a particular favorite of the Wilsons." His mother smiled at the memory. "This is going to be so much fun. I'll look through my cookbook tomorrow and see what else I can come up with."

She went back to her crocheting, and he and Elise exchanged a smile. He had a feeling they both were of one mind. Whatever they could do to keep his mother this happy and active, they would strive to do.

"Son?"

Derrick pulled his gaze away from Elise to find his mother's glance going back and forth between the two of them. "Yes, ma'am?"

"When you go into town tomorrow to talk to the preacher, would you see if you can get ahold of some of this white yarn? I can cut you off a piece so it will be easy for you to match."

"I'll try to find you some."

"Good. That baby will need a blanket, too."

࿇

Harold Burton did indeed know of a couple of families who were struggling to get by this year. He wrote down the names and ages of the children in each family and handed the slip of paper to Derrick. "This is a good thing you're doing, Derrick. I know the Ballards and the Hansons will be more than a little appreciative."

"Well, the Lord has blessed me greatly this year. I feel I should be giving to others."

"I'm sure the Lord will continue to bless you with that attitude, son."

Derrick began to shake his head. That wasn't why he was doing this.

"I know you aren't doing it to get anything back, Derrick," Harold said as if he knew what Derrick was thinking. "We both understand that we can't work our way to heaven. Still, we're to do the work the Lord puts before us, and He certainly knows a good deed when He sees it."

"It makes me feel good to be able to give to those less fortunate. But I suspect that most of them would just as soon not need the help."

"That's true. Most people would rather be in a position to give." Harold nodded and stood up to shake hands as Derrick stood and stuffed the list into his pocket. "God bless you, son. We'll see you on Sunday."

"See you then."

Derrick had a feeling his mother and Elise were both going to be even more excited once they knew they could help make Christmas special for the Ballard and Hanson families. As for him, he felt more blessed than ever knowing that he didn't have to spend this Christmas alone. It had been so long since he'd spent the holiday with family.

He stopped at the mercantile to see if he could find the yarn his mother wanted and was glad to find that they had several skeins in stock. He bought two of them to take home to her. The shopkeeper was getting in new items for Christmas, and just seeing him put a doll in the window made Derrick feel like a child again. He found that his mother and Elise wouldn't be the only ones getting excited about helping these families out. If he wasn't mistaken, there was a little girl on his list who would probably love that doll.

He checked to make sure and then asked for a doll just like the one on display. One gift bought and many more to go. As he tied the packages onto his horse, Derrick realized that he probably should have waited and asked the women in his home about the doll. He certainly didn't want them to miss out on the fun, but he was afraid the dolls would all be gone before he got back into town. As Derrick headed home with his purchases, he couldn't wait to tell them about how their plans to give goodies had grown into something much bigger.

When he rode up to his house, he was pleasantly surprised to find Jed's horse and wagon tied to his hitching rail out front. Derrick forgot his packages for the moment and hurried inside to find Jed and Caroline sitting at the kitchen table visiting with his mother and Elise.

"Here is Derrick now," his mother said as he entered the kitchen. "Look who has come to see us."

"Jed, Caroline, it's good to see you. How are you feeling, Caroline?"

"Like a whale," she said, laughing good-naturedly.

Derrick knew enough not to comment about that and was glad that Jed did, too.

"You look beautiful to me," Jed told his wife. He looked at Derrick and grinned. "Doc says we may have our baby anytime now. Caroline wanted to check with your mother and Elise to see if they had any advice for us for when it's time. Doc said he would be coming out the next few days to check on her, but what if things start to happen in the middle of the night? I need to know what to do."

"I've told him to bring her here at the first sign of labor, Derrick. That way you could go for the doctor and he could stay with Caroline. Also, Elise and I would be here to help."

Derrick wasn't quite sure how he felt about that until he looked at Jed. He could see that the man was concerned about having to leave Caroline alone. He'd feel the same way if it were his wife. "That sounds like a good plan to me, Jed."

The younger man let his breath out in one giant whoosh. "Thank you, Derrick. Caroline has taken to your mother and Elise, and with no women relatives around. . . Well, it makes us both feel better to know we have someone nearby who knows about these things."

Derrick nodded. He could understand that. "I'm glad we're here, too. And glad Mama and Elise are here to know what to do—if needed. It's for sure that I don't."

Elise and his mother convinced the young couple to stay for supper, and Caroline pitched in and helped finish it up while Jed went out to help Derrick with his evening chores.

"I can't tell you how much it means to Caroline and me to have you all to turn to," Jed said as he took the bridle off Derrick's horse for him. "She's been missin' her mama something awful. But ever since Thanksgiving, she's felt better. It kind of felt like being with family to be over here with you all."

"We enjoyed having you two with us, Jed. And I'm glad that my mama and Elise have made a difference to Caroline."

"I'll sure be glad when this baby gets here. I can tell you, I'm plumb nervous about it all."

Derrick's heart went out to the younger man. "I'd be just as anxious as you," he assured Jed. "And I doubt there's a man out there who wouldn't feel the same way."

"You think so?"

"I do."

Jed only nodded, but he seemed to relax just a bit. By the

time they went back to the house, supper was ready. Derrick brought his packages in and put them in the pantry for the time being.

He half expected that they'd eat in the dining room. Instead, they all gathered around the kitchen table, and after he said the blessing, they shared a meal of beef stew and Elise's fluffy biscuits.

"This tastes so good to me," Caroline said. "I guess I'm just getting tired of my own cooking."

"You're probably just plain tired, dear," Derrick's mother said.

"Well, whatever it is, it sure is nice to taste someone else's cooking. I'll repay you after the baby gets here."

"We'd love to come over for supper one night after you have the baby, but not until you're up to it."

Caroline nodded. "Soon as I am, though."

"We'd be glad to come then," Elise assured her.

They sat and talked for a while after supper, but even Derrick could tell Caroline was tiring fast when Jed suggested that they leave.

"You be sure and bring her over here first sign of that baby coming, Jed, you hear?" Frieda said.

"Oh yes, ma'am. You don't have to worry about that." Jed chuckled.

As they waved the young couple good-bye, Derrick had a feeling they'd see them again in a day or two—if not sooner. "Do you think she's going to have the baby soon, Mama?"

"Oh, I think so. It wouldn't surprise me a bit if we saw them again tonight. We probably should have had them just stay here until the baby comes."

"Do you want me to go after them?"

"No. It'll be better for them to decide what to do, son." She turned to go back into the house.

Derrick looked at Elise. He wasn't sure his mother was making sense.

"They'll grow closer as a couple through all this if they're the ones deciding when they need help and when they don't," Elise explained.

Derrick nodded. He thought he understood now, and as he followed Elise inside, a sudden wave of longing washed over him. . .for his deepest dreams to come true. But he'd been dreaming the same thing for a very long time. It would be only with the Lord's help that he had any hope of it coming true. But it sure seemed to be taking Him a long time to show Derrick what to do.

ten

With all the excitement over Caroline and Jed's baby coming soon, it was the next morning before Elise thought to ask Derrick about his trip to town. "What did you find out from the preacher, Derrick?" she asked as she dished up breakfast.

"He gave me the names of two families who could use some help this year. I'm not sure I know them." He took his plate and his mother's and brought them to the table. "Have either of you met the Ballard or Hanson families?"

His mother shook her head. "I don't believe so. What about you, Elise? Do those names sound familiar?"

Elise joined them at the table with her own plate and the coffeepot. "I think I might have met the Ballards. I seem to recall a couple who had three children coming up to me a few weeks ago at church. I believe their last name was Ballard. I can't remember their first names, though. I'm terrible at that."

Derrick looked at the list of names while Elise warmed up his coffee. "That might have been them. The Ballards have three children—Anna, who is six; Benjamin, nine; and Luke, twelve."

Elise took her seat and nodded. "I think it was two boys and a little girl. They were very well mannered. The little girl had a really sweet smile."

Derrick suddenly jumped up from the table and hurried into the pantry. He came back with two packages wrapped in brown paper. "I almost forgot these. Mama, here is your yarn. They have a few more skeins of white if you need it. And they have a lot of other colors in stock."

"Thank you, son," his mother said, taking the yarn from him. "I just ran out of what I had yesterday. I can finish the blanket now. What's that other package you have there?"

"Well, ordinarily I wouldn't have bought this without talking to the two of you first, but the shopkeeper was just putting them out, and I didn't want to take the chance that he might sell out before I got back in there." He carefully unwrapped the doll and held it up. It had blue eyes and blond hair and rosy cheeks. "Do you think this is something young Anna might like?"

"Oh, Derrick, it's perfect." Elise took it from him and turned it this way and that before handing it to his mother. "Nearly every little girl dreams of getting a doll just like this for Christmas."

"It's lovely, son. I'm glad you went ahead and bought it. As pretty as it is, it might have been taken. Now tell us what you want to do for these families."

Derrick sat back down at the table and took a sip of coffee before answering. "Well, I'd love to make this a wonderful Christmas for them. But I'd like to help them get through some tough times, too. It can't be easy to raise a family when hard times are on you. I need to give more thought to what I might do there, but in the meantime, I think we need to plan on buying presents for the children and maybe providing the makings for Christmas dinner."

"That sounds great. But that's mostly buying things. What about the baked goods and candy we'd planned on giving out?" his mother asked.

"Oh, I want us to take that to them, as well. . .and to the neighbors around here, too."

"Good, good." Frieda nodded her head. "Well then, we

need to start listing ideas for gifts and what we want to buy for their Christmas dinner, and then decide what all we'll be cooking to give out."

"We need your list of neighbors and friends, too, Derrick," Elise reminded him.

"I'll make up that list today. Oh, and another thing—I'd kind of like the help we give the families to be anonymous. I don't want them feeling beholden to us."

Elise's heart turned to pure mush. Derrick was a wonderful man. The more she got to know him, the more deeply she cared for him. "I love that idea. Maybe you could give the things we get to Preacher Burton and he could see that they get them? Then the parents could put the gifts under the tree and the children wouldn't have to know that they couldn't afford to get them on their own."

Derrick grinned at her, sending her pulse racing. "That's what I was thinking, too. I'm glad you agree."

Elise looked over at Frieda and found her gaze going back and forth between Derrick and her. Her mother-in-law smiled at the two of them. "You two think an awful lot alike. I think that's the right thing to do, too. The pleasure comes from the giving and knowing it was put to good use, not from making people feel they owe you."

They'd just finished eating breakfast and had begun to make their lists when a loud pounding came at the back door. "Derrick!"

"That's Jed's voice!" Derrick said, hurrying to the door.

Elise jumped to her feet and was by his side when he opened it to find Jed standing there holding up his wife, who was obviously in labor.

"I've got to go get Doc! The baby is coming, and you said to bring Caroline over first thing."

"Yes, we did," Derrick said, moving away from the door so that Jed could bring his wife inside.

Elise quickly decided what to do. "I'll go up and turn my bed down. Can you carry her up, Jed?"

"I can." He swept his wife up into his arms and followed Elise up the stairs. She'd barely pulled the covers down when he laid his wife down as gently as possible. "I'm going after the doc, Caroline."

"No," Derrick said from the doorway, where he stood with his mother. "You stay with your wife, and I'll go get Doc."

"Are you sure?" Jed asked.

Elise could see from the grip that Caroline had on her husband's hand that she didn't want him to go anywhere. So, evidently, could Derrick.

"I'm sure. I think Caroline would much rather have you by her side right now than me."

"Thank you, Derrick."

Derrick nodded and turned quickly to go back downstairs.

"I'll go get some water on to boil and get some fresh linens and bring them up," Elise told Frieda.

Her mother-in-law nodded. "Jed and I will try to make Caroline as comfortable as possible." She leaned over and whispered, "Tell Derrick to hurry."

Elise nodded and hurried downstairs just as Derrick grabbed his jacket from a hook beside the door and pulled it on. "Mama said to tell you to hurry."

"I will. I'm hoping I'll run into Doc on his way to their place. Tell them I'll get him back here soon as I can. And pray that I don't miss him."

"I will," Elise said as she saw him out the door.

Then she put the teakettle and a big pot of water on to boil. She hurried back upstairs and gathered some clean towels and linens and took them to her room. Jed was on one side of the bed and Frieda was on the other. Caroline's color was a bit better, and she seemed to be in between labor pains at the moment.

"Thank you for letting me use your room, Elise," Caroline said, sounding a little breathless.

"You're quite welcome. Derrick said to tell you that he would hurry to get Doc back here."

"Good." Caroline began to breathe shallowly, and Elise could tell another pain was on its way.

The pains seemed to come more often and last longer as the clock ticked the minutes away. Hard as she tried to keep from showing it, Elise couldn't help but be apprehensive. Her labor had been similar to Caroline's, only her child had been stillborn. Memories sent tears flooding to her eyes, and Elise blinked quickly, trying to keep them from falling. She turned toward the door. "I'm going to see about the water."

"Yes, dear," Frieda said softly and nodded. "I'll call if we need you."

Elise hurried out of the room. This was a joyous time for Jed and Caroline, and she didn't want to put a damper on it with her painful memories. There were other things she should be doing. She dropped to her knees at one of the chairs and prayed. *Dear Lord, please watch over Caroline and the baby. Please let Doc get here soon, and please, please, dear Lord, let the baby be all right. In Jesus' name I pray. Amen.*

The teakettle began to whistle, and Elise hurried to push it to the back of the stove. Just then the back door opened and Derrick and Doc entered.

"I found Doc," Derrick said. "He was on his way to Jed's."

"Oh, I am so glad. I think it's about time," Elise said.

"I'll show him the way up," Derrick said, leading the doctor through the house and up the stairs.

Elise sent up a prayer of thanksgiving that Derrick had been able to find the doctor. "And please let this baby be born soon and be healthy, and please let Caroline be all right, dear Lord," she whispered.

❧

Derrick came back downstairs to find Elise making a pot of tea. She looked as if she'd been about to cry when he and Doc had come into the room, and he couldn't help but wonder why. He crossed the room to stand behind her. "Elise, are you all right?"

"I'm fine." She didn't turn around, and he was pretty sure he heard a sniffle.

Derrick put his hands on her arms and gently turned her to face him, but she wouldn't look at him. "What is it? What can I do?"

She shook her head, and Derrick reached out to tip her chin so he could see her face. Her eyes were swimming with unshed tears. "Please tell me. Let me help."

Suddenly her face was burrowed in his shoulder and she was sobbing. "I just pray everything is all right with the baby and Caroline."

"I'm sure it will be. Doc is here now, and he'll take care of things," Derrick said, rubbing her back. He didn't know what to do. He just wanted her to quit crying. He could feel her nod, but she didn't lift her head.

"Elise, this is more than just concern. Please tell me what's wrong. Please."

She took a deep breath and brushed at the tears that began to stream down her face. She shook her head. "I'm just a little. . .worried. I thought everything. . .was fine when it was time for mine. . .and Carl's baby to be born."

She choked up, and Derrick felt as if the breath had been

knocked clean out of him. How could he have forgotten that Elise and Carl had lost their baby? "I'm so sorry, Elise. This must be very stressful for you."

"I just want them both to be all right. I don't want Caroline and Jed to have to go through that kind of pain."

She began to cry again, and he pulled her closer into his arms, rocking her back and forth. "I'm sure they'll be fine, Elise. Doc is here, and—"

The sound of a baby's cry could be heard from the top of the stairs. Elise pulled back, and the smile on her face was one Derrick knew he would never forget.

"The baby is here. And it's. . .crying. It's all right!" Elise turned and rushed to the stairs. Derrick hurried up right behind her. But outside the door she paused and wiped at her tears with her apron while Derrick knocked to make sure it was all right for them to enter.

"Come on in," Jed called.

Elise took a deep breath before opening the door to her room.

Mother and baby were indeed fine. They entered the room to find Caroline propped up on several pillows, holding her brand-new baby. Jed was sitting on the bed beside her, the baby's tiny fist in his hand.

Standing right behind Elise, Derrick put his hand on her shoulder and gave it a squeeze. She reached up and patted it as if she knew that he was trying to comfort her in the only way he could at the moment.

"Come see, Elise," his mother said, motioning Elise on into the room. "Doc says baby Jonathan is beautiful and very healthy."

Derrick was pretty sure his mother was aware of what Elise had been going through downstairs.

Elise moved away from him and over to the side of the bed. He couldn't see her face, but he could hear her voice.

"Oh, Caroline. . .he's gorgeous," Elise said.

❧

The next week was a bevy of activity at Derrick's house. His mother and Elise insisted that Jed, Caroline, and the baby stay with them until Caroline had regained her strength. After his mother and Elise assured him that they didn't mind sleeping in the same room until the young couple went home, Derrick readily agreed.

Elise was sure he didn't mind, but he seemed a little unsettled that their normal routine had changed. He never griped about it, though. After breakfast each day, Jed would go to his place and take care of things there while Derrick did the same at home, leaving the house to the women and the newborn baby most of the day.

When Derrick did come inside, he never complained if a meal was a little late getting to the table or if he had to come upstairs to find them. Elise was a little concerned that all the going up and down stairs and the busier pace of the days might take their toll on her mother-in-law, but Frieda assured her that she loved every minute of it.

And Elise had no doubt that she meant every word. More often than not, when Caroline was napping, Frieda could be found humming a tune and rocking the baby in the rocking chair in the corner of the room. What a wonderful grandmother she would have made had her and Carl's baby lived. Then Elise fought off the sorrowful memories and went back downstairs without disturbing the two.

Her own workload had doubled, but she didn't mind. She liked taking care of people, and, especially right now, it gave her less time to think about her crying episode the day the baby was born.

Elise had felt a little uncomfortable around Derrick ever since that day, but it wasn't because of Derrick's treatment of her. It was because she couldn't forget how wonderful it had felt to be held in his arms.

Now, as he entered the kitchen, her heart seemed to do a funny little dip and flip. She tried to will it to beat as normal, but that had become nearly impossible when Derrick was around.

"It's awfully quiet this time of day. Are Caroline and the baby napping?" he asked as he poured himself a cup of coffee.

"I think so. They were a little while ago."

"Where's Mama?"

Elise chuckled. "She may be napping, too, by now. But last I saw her she was humming to a sleeping baby."

"She's enjoying herself, isn't she?"

"Yes, she is." Elise nodded. "I think she's going to miss all the hustle and bustle when they go back home."

"I'm afraid of that, too. But with Christmas coming, and all the plans we need to finish making, maybe she won't miss them too much. We'll just have to keep her interest up in everything else." Derrick finished his coffee. "Do you need me to bring anything in from the pantry or root cellar before I go back out?"

It warmed Elise's heart that Derrick asked her if there was something he could do for her at least once a day. "You could bring in potatoes if you would."

He went to get them right away and placed them on the worktable.

"Thank you."

"No. Thank *you*, Elise. You've been working tirelessly these past few days. I thank you for all you do for us all."

She could feel the color rush up her neck and into her cheeks at his words. "You're welcome, but it's something I enjoy doing."

"That makes it even better. I'm going to be working close by. If you need anything, just yell."

"I will. Thank you."

It was several minutes after he left the room before her heartbeat slowed back to normal. She should be getting used to its erratic behavior by now, but it never failed to surprise her. Elise had never thought she'd feel like this again. She'd never thought she could care about anyone other than Carl. But it seemed she was wrong. She was falling more deeply in love with his brother with each passing day.

᠉

Later that night, when Jed and Caroline announced that they would be going back to their place the next day, Derrick couldn't say he was disappointed. They'd been there well-nigh a week.

"Are you sure you're up to going home?" his mother asked Caroline.

"I think so. You and Elise have helped me so very much. And, Derrick, Jed and I appreciate you welcoming us into your home like you did. I can't begin to tell you all how much it's meant to us." The tears in the young woman's eyes told them even more than her words.

"I can't thank you enough for taking care of Caroline and the baby like you have," Jed said. "Not to mention that you've fed us all and. . . Well, if you ever need us for anything at all, just know that we will be there."

"You've become family to us, and we just love you all," Caroline added.

"You've become like family to us, too, you know," Elise said.

"And that baby of yours. . . Well, we feel we have a claim on little Jonathan now, you know?" Derrick's mother said. "It's going to be real lonely around here with you gone."

"You come over anytime, Miss Frieda."

"What about Christmas? You'll spend it here with us, won't you?" Frieda asked.

"Why, that is so wonderful of you. We would love to—"

"But I'm afraid we won't be able to," Jed said, interrupting his wife's acceptance.

"Jed—"

Jed smiled at his wife. "I was saving this for a surprise, Caroline. But I can tell I'd better let you know about it now. Remember I telegraphed your mama and papa about the baby?"

Caroline nodded. "Yes."

"Well, I went into town today and we had an answer back from them. They're coming out here for Christmas. They can't wait to see you and their grandson."

Caroline caught her breath just before she began to cry. "They're coming here? Mama and Papa?" she asked through her tears.

Jed nodded, looking confused. "I thought you'd be happy about it."

"Oh, Jed. I *am* happy! I just never thought my parents would make the long trip out here." Caroline cuddled her son to her breast and dropped a kiss on his head. "I can't wait for them to see the baby and our place."

Derrick smile at the young couple. They were happy to be going home, and he would be glad for things to get back to normal. He'd been missing the routine he and Elise and his mother had developed. But he was glad they'd been able to help the young couple.

eleven

Both Elise and his mother seemed a bit lost right after Jed bundled his wife and son up and took them back to their place. Elise reclaimed her room and spent most of the afternoon getting it back to normal while his mother pulled out her crochet work, wanting to get finished with the blanket she'd barely started for little Jonathan.

Even Derrick had to admit that the house seemed more than a little quiet after Jed and Caroline and the baby went home, but he wasn't complaining. It wasn't until that evening, though, when Elise was making supper and his mother set the table for three, that things seemed to be returning to normal.

"Your workload should be a little easier now," Derrick said to Elise as she fried potatoes to go with the beans she'd put on earlier.

"Yes, it will be," Elise said, carefully turning the potatoes. "But it's going to seem a little lonely without that sweet baby."

"Yes, it is. And I do miss them already, I admit it," his mother added. "But Jed and Caroline need to be in their own place and leaning on each other. Besides, they don't live that far away. I can get you to take me over there if I get to missing that baby too much, can't I, son?"

"I'll be glad to take you over anytime, Mama. I know you both miss the hustle and bustle of having houseguests, and especially the baby. But I have to tell you, I'm kind of glad things are getting back to normal."

"Why, son, I never knew you were missing our company so," his mother said, patting him on the back.

"Well, I was." Derrick couldn't believe he'd let those word escape his lips. But they were true. He'd missed his mother's and Elise's company. They'd been so busy taking care of their guests, he'd barely had a conversation with them the last few days. "I guess you've spoiled me."

"Well, you can have our undivided attention tonight, can't he, Elise?"

Derrick watched the delicate color flood Elise's face. His mother had kind of put her on the spot, and for a moment he thought she wasn't going to answer. Then she smiled and said, "Only if he makes cocoa for us."

"Consider it done," Derrick said, agreeing to the terms.

❧

The next morning, his mother and Elise still seemed a little down until Derrick reminded them they had some unfinished business to take care of. "You know we're a little behind on our Christmas plans. I know that our guests had to take precedence while they were here, but it's time we get back to planning what we're going to do."

Elise looked at the calendar. "You're right. We've only got a little over two weeks until Christmas!"

"My, I didn't realize we were that far into December," his mother said. "Let's get those lists made up."

Derrick pulled out the names the preacher had given him, and Elise got some paper and pencils and brought them to the table.

"We have the doll for Anna. I was thinking maybe a sling-shot for Benjamin, but I'm not sure what to get Luke," he said.

"Wouldn't they both like a slingshot?" his mother asked. "You and Carl liked them at twelve."

"We did, didn't we? That would make it easier. And then I thought maybe some books?"

"I've heard that *The Red Badge of Courage* by Stephen Crane is very good. The boys might enjoy it," Elise said. "And maybe Anna would enjoy *Black Beauty* by Anna Sewell. If she can't read yet, I'm sure someone in the family will enjoy reading it out loud to her."

"Yes, those are good suggestions, Elise. Thank you." Derrick wrote them down.

"What about clothes—do they need those, Derrick?"

Derrick sighed and shook his head. "Mama, I didn't think to ask. I'll check with Harold next time I go into town. He'll know. Now, what about the Hanson family? They have two girls—one fifteen and one sixteen. I'm not sure what they might like."

Elise looked thoughtful before she answered. "At that age, most likely, clothes, even if they don't need them. Or I'm sure they'd like a parasol, a reticule, or maybe a pretty shawl for winter."

Derrick's mother nodded. "Those are all good suggestions, Elise. I wish I had your sewing machine right now. I could sure put it to good use here."

"I wish we had it, too, Mama," Elise said.

Derrick suddenly knew what he was getting his mother for Christmas. He hoped the mercantile carried sewing machines. If not, he could order one from the Sears & Roebuck catalog, but he wasn't sure he could get it on time. Maybe Elise could go into town with him and show him what to buy.

"Will you be getting anything for the parents, Derrick?" his mother asked.

"Well, I'd like to help them out monetarily, but I'm not sure how to go about that."

"Could you put some cash in an envelope? Or maybe pay for a line of credit at the mercantile?" Elise suggested.

"Oh, that's an excellent suggestion, Elise. I'll definitely look into the line of credit. If it's possible, I think I'll have Harold take care of it so that no one knows."

"I'm sure he'd be glad to help you out in that way," his mother said.

Derrick nodded, pleased with the way their plans were coming along. "I'm sure he will."

"We still need that list from you of neighbors and friends."

"I can start making that now."

Elise slid him a sheet of paper and handed him a pencil and then got up to get his mother's cookbook. "Here, Mama. Look through this and see if there are any new recipes you want us to try out. I'll go take stock of what we have in the panty."

Derrick smiled as he worked on his list. Finally, things were really getting back to normal.

&

Elise was just finishing her inventory when Derrick came into the pantry. Her heart skittered at his nearness.

"How's your list going?" he asked.

"It's a big one that will probably get longer once I talk to Mama and see what she's come up with to try out."

"Would you go into town with me today or tomorrow to make sure I get everything and help me pick out some presents?" His voice changed to a whisper. "I particularly need you to help me with Mama's present. I know what I want to get her, but I'd like your advice about it."

Elise peeked into the kitchen to see Frieda going over the cookbook. "What are you thinking of buying her?"

"I want to get her a sewing machine."

"Oh, Derrick, she's going to love that! I'll be glad to go with you. But what if she wants to come along?"

"Then we can just take her with us and plan another outing to get her present then."

"Does the mercantile carry sewing machines?"

"I don't know. If not, I'll order from the catalog and just wrap up a picture for her if it doesn't get here in time."

Elise chuckled. "That would work."

"I just don't want to wait too long. I'd like to make sure I get the things on our list for the Hansons and the Ballards while there's still a good selection."

"I can go either day—whichever one is best for you."

"Let's go see how far along Mama is with her list."

As Elise followed Derrick back into the kitchen, she found she was looking forward to the outing very much. She needed to do a little shopping herself. With all their talk of lists, she thought Derrick might enjoy a book to read in the evenings this winter. And she had a feeling his mother would be happy with a lot of yarn and maybe a few new crochet pattern books.

"Mama, do you have your list finished? I thought Elise and I might go into town and buy the staples and other supplies you two will need for your baking and candy making. And I thought I'd go ahead and get some of those presents on our list. You can come along, too, of course."

"No, I don't think I'm quite up to a trip to town after all that's been going on lately. I'll let the two of you go. I'll be fine here."

"Are you sure?"

"Yes. I want to finish the blanket for little Jonathan. You can pick me up some more yarn, though. I'd like several skeins of black, and some of red, if they have them."

"They did last time I was in. We'll get them for you."

Frieda handed her list to Elise. "These are some ingredients we'll need for a few new recipes I found. I didn't know if we had them or not."

Elise glanced over the list. "Some of them we do, but I'll pick up the rest today. We can start trying some of the new recipes out tonight or tomorrow."

"Oh, one other thing I've been thinking of. Derrick, I don't suppose you've put up a Christmas tree since you've been here?"

"No, Mama, I haven't."

"Well, we can make popcorn garlands and that kind of thing, but you might look at decorations if you plan on cutting a tree this year."

"I'll see what's available." Derrick poured himself a fresh cup of coffee and turned to Elise. "How long do you think it will take to get ready?"

"What about dinner for you, Mama? Should we wait until afternoon to go?"

Frieda shook her head. "I'm perfectly capable to see to my own dinner. We have beans I can heat up from last night, and there are biscuits from this morning. You two go on and have dinner in town somewhere. I'll be fine."

"You're sure?"

"I'm certain. Go. Have a good time shopping."

Elise looked at Derrick. "I just need to freshen up. That won't take but a few minutes."

"I'll go get the wagon and bring it over, then."

Elise ran up the stairs feeling almost like a schoolgirl. She hurriedly freshened up, straightened her hair, and went back down the stairs as fast as she could.

Derrick had just entered the kitchen. "Are you ready?"

"I am. I just need to grab my cloak."

"You'd better take mine, dear. It's a mite heavier than what you brought down from Denver."

"Thank you, Mama. It will be much warmer than mine." She really hadn't planned on staying this long and didn't have the wardrobe for wintertime. But she'd been making do. She could do so awhile longer. This past week had shown that Mama was getting back to her old self, and Elise knew she needed to get back to Denver. She didn't want to think about it now—in fact, she didn't want to think about it at all. She was aware that she wasn't going to be able to put it off for much longer, but she wasn't going to think about it today. She was going to enjoy this outing with Derrick. It might never happen again.

❧

Derrick couldn't believe Elise had agreed to go into town with him. Ever since the day she'd cried in his arms, he had a feeling she was uncomfortable around him. He'd tried to act as normal as possible, but he didn't know how much longer he was going to be able to hide how he felt about her.

It'd been all he could do today, when they were both in the pantry and standing so near each other, not to pull her into his arms and tell her he loved her. But with her acting so skittish around him, he wasn't sure at all what her reaction would be. She might decide to head back to Denver right away.

That was the last thing he wanted, and it was fear of losing her that had him trying to be patient. Part of him just wanted things to go on like they were, with Elise growing to love him one day. But being around Jed and Caroline had made him long for a loving relationship like theirs, and he was getting impatient to have a family of his own. Waiting on the Lord to show him what to do was getting harder all the time.

"Where are we going first?" Elise asked as he helped her into the wagon.

"I think we should pay the preacher a visit and then have some dinner," he said, making sure she had the lap robe pulled up. He hurried around and took his seat beside her and flipped the reins. "We can do our shopping after that. How does that sound to you?"

"It sounds fine," Elise said. She took a deep breath of cold air and blew it back out, giggling when she saw the vapor it left.

She watched the scenery go by with interest, and Derrick could tell she was enjoying the ride. He felt bad that he hadn't taken her on more outings.

Between taking care of his mother, the house, and then Jed and Caroline, there hadn't been much free time for her. He'd have to see what he could do about that in the future.

When they arrived at the Burton house, Harold and Rachel welcomed them into their home and kitchen.

"What brings you two out today?" Rachel asked as she poured them both a cup of coffee.

"Well, I talked to Harold a week or so ago about doing something for a few of the families around, and we came for more information and to ask a favor," Derrick said.

"What do you need to know, Derrick?" the preacher asked.

After Derrick explained what they were doing and what he wanted to do to help in a monetary way, Rachel had tears in her eyes. "The children are going to love the things you want to get them. As for the line of credit at the mercantile, well, that's just a wonderful idea."

"That was Elise's suggestion," Derrick said.

Elise shook her head. "Derrick wanted his gift to be

anonymous, and that just seemed an answer to how he could keep it that way."

"We all agreed that we don't want them to know where the gifts come from. If I could have kept it from you two, I would have," Derrick said, grinning at the preacher before continuing, "but I need your help in getting the presents to them. And, Harold. . .I would like it if I could give you the money and you could pay for the line of credit at the mercantile. You could let them know that they have it, but that way the families wouldn't feel they had to pay it back or have to feel beholden to anyone."

The preacher and his wife exchanged glances. "We've just come from visiting the Barristers," Harold said. "They told us you opened your home to them, Derrick, and they mentioned how much your mother and Elise here helped Caroline. It's a blessing to see Christian values put into action. We'd be glad to help you out with your plans for Christmas. Be more than happy to."

The Burtons asked them to stay for dinner, but Derrick wanted to treat Elise to a meal at the hotel dining room. She'd seemed to enjoy it when he'd taken her and his mother before.

"Thank you, but we have shopping to do yet, and we don't want to leave Mama alone too long."

They said their good-byes, then Derrick helped Elise back onto the wagon seat. "We're off to have dinner at the Grand Hotel, and then we'll get to our shopping."

"Derrick, we could have eaten with the Burtons. It would have saved you some money."

"I know—and I'm sure we would have enjoyed it—but I want to take you out for something special. You deserve it."

❧

Elise was more than a little pleased that Derrick wanted to

take her to dinner at the hotel. She'd enjoyed it a lot when they'd gone there before. It did have a special feeling to her. Maybe it was because she could order whatever she wanted and have it brought to her. And she didn't have to worry about cleaning up.

She was sure the meal at the Burtons' would have been very good. But they'd just dropped in on the couple, and Elise was sure they hadn't planned to have company for dinner if they'd just returned from Jed and Caroline's. She hadn't wanted Rachel to go out of her way. Besides, she would have felt the need to help in the kitchen, and that would have held them up with the shopping they needed to do. It would have been fine, but she was very pleased that Derrick had kept to his original plans.

Derrick pulled the wagon near a hitching post close to the hotel and hooked the reins around the post. He helped Elise down and pulled her hand through his arm as they made their way to the hotel dining room. It was nothing any of the other gentlemen escorting ladies into the room weren't doing, but it made Elise's pulse race once more. As they were seated across from one another, her heart was pounding so hard, she could hear it. She was thankful of conversations going on in the room so that Derrick couldn't.

The special of the day was stuffed pork chops with lyonnaise potatoes, served with hot rolls and a choice of dessert—peach cobbler or apple dumplings. The meal was truly good and not just because she got tired of her own cooking from time to time.

"This is all wonderful," she said as she cut another piece of her apple dumpling—her choice for dessert.

"The Grand Hotel started out as a boardinghouse," Derrick said. "Through the past few years they've gained a reputation for serving fine food."

"I can certainly see why. Everything is delicious. Thank you for bringing me."

"You're more than welcome. Thank you for accompanying me. I ate here often before you and Mama came. But it was never quite so enjoyable as today."

"I'm sure there are several single women in the area who would be more than glad to have dinner with you, Derrick. I'm curious as to why you never married." Elise inhaled quickly. She couldn't believe those words had actually left her mouth.

"Are you sure you want to know?"

"I'm sorry, Derrick. It's really none of my business," she apologized.

Derrick smiled across the table at her. "Perhaps not. But maybe it's time you know. There's only one woman I ever thought seriously about courting."

"Oh?"

"Yes. I was attracted to her for a very long time. But I didn't act fast enough."

"What happened?"

"She married my brother."

Elise could feel the color flood her cheeks as she realized she was the woman he was talking about. "Oh! Derrick, I don't know what to say. I never knew about your feelings for me."

"As I said, I wasn't fast enough. Carl was."

"I—"

"It's all right, Elise. You were happy with Carl, and I know he had to be a happy man—married to you. I didn't mean to upset you. You asked about it, and I just thought it was time you knew."

"I—thank you for telling me." Elise's heart was pounding

against her ribs so hard it almost hurt. Should she tell him that she'd hoped he would ask to court her long before Carl did? No. That seemed too disloyal to Carl. And yet. . .he'd been honest with her. To keep herself from acting before thinking things over, she forced herself to take another bite of her dumpling. She was relieved when Derrick seemed to sense her discomfort and changed the subject.

"Do you really think Mama will be happy with a sewing machine?"

He smiled at her, and Elise felt herself relax. "Oh, I'm certain of it."

"I'm glad you came with me today. I don't know a thing about sewing machines, and I need your advice."

"I'm glad to give it to you. There are several different kinds out there. I have a Singer and I love it, but there are others that are good, too. Sears & Roebuck carries other brands. We'll just see what we can find. Mama is going to be thrilled—whether she gets it Christmas morning or has to wait a little while if you have to order it. She's wanted one of her own for a long time. She's a very good seamstress, but having a sewing machine will make it so much easier for her."

"Good. I'm glad she seems to be doing better. Having Jed and Caroline and the baby really did perk her up. She seems to be doing well now."

"Yes, she does. I pray she continues to." Elise held her breath, waiting to see if Derrick was going to suggest that she could feel free to go back to Denver, but he didn't. She knew she should bring it up, but she couldn't bring herself to do so. Surely all of that could wait until after Christmas. Surely it could.

twelve

As they finished their meal and left to go shopping, Derrick was glad he'd finally let Elise know he'd wanted to court her before his brother beat him to it. It was something he'd lived with for so long, and somehow, when she'd given him an opening, he felt it was the right time to tell her. He could only pray he was right. Maybe it was the expression in her eyes when he'd told her, but he had hope that maybe now she would begin to think of him as more than just Carl's brother.

Derrick couldn't remember when he'd ever had such fun shopping. With Elise at his side, the day was more enjoyable than any he'd had in a long while. They had to go to both mercantile stores in town to find the right sewing machine for his mother.

He'd never have been able to decide if Elise hadn't been with him. They all looked the same to him, but Elise knew what she was looking for. Neither store had any Singer sewing machines in stock, but Elise looked closely at what they did carry and found one she thought would be just as good.

She convinced the storekeeper to let her try it out, and when all was said and done, she'd found one she thought his mother would love.

"Its stitching is every bit as good as my machine—maybe better because it's newer. It's very nicely made and easy to thread. I've heard the Minnesota is a very good machine, and it appears to be. Sears & Roebuck carries it, too. I think your mother is going to love the walnut cabinet with all those drawers. It's beautiful."

"I ordered this machine in from Sears & Roebuck," the storekeeper said. "With Christmas coming, I always sell several."

"Do you think I should wait and try to get a Singer?" Derrick asked.

"No," Elise said, standing firm in her choice. "I think this machine is as good as my own. I know I'd be happy with it."

That was all it took to convince Derrick. He asked the shopkeeper to box it up for him and went to the counter to pay. "I'll bring my wagon back in a little while."

Elise looked around while he paid for the sewing machine, which gave Derrick a chance to buy her present, too. "Do you have that wool cloak there in the display window in a size that would fit the young woman who helped me with the machine?" he asked.

The shopkeeper looked over at Elise and nodded. "I'm sure I do. If it doesn't fit, you can bring it back."

"But it's a Christmas present, so it'd be after then before I'd bring it back if it's the wrong size."

"Doesn't matter. I'll take it back or get you another one if it doesn't fit."

"Good. Add it to the sewing machine, then. I may make more purchases later, but I'll pay for those two items now." Elise was coming his way, so he quickly paid the man. "I'll pick them up in an hour or so."

The man nodded as he took the cash from Derrick and handed him a receipt. "See you in a while."

Derrick met Elise halfway up the aisle and asked, "Did you find anything else on our list?"

She nodded. "I found a few things. But I think we need to

go back to the other store. I saw several items there for the children and the older girls. And I think they have the books we wanted to get."

"Let's go." Derrick felt good about getting presents for the two most important women in his life. He'd never looked forward to Christmas quite so much in his life.

At the other store, they handed their list of staples and goods they needed for all the cooking to a salesclerk. Then they went to look for presents while he was filling the order.

This store did have what they wanted for the Hansons and the Ballards. For the Hanson girls they bought the reticules Elise had suggested—one in black trimmed in gold for Margaret, and one in gold trimmed in black for Jennifer. They even found matching parasols to go with them.

"Oh, look at this, Derrick," Elise said, showing him a bag of marbles. "Do you think the boys would like these?"

"I'm sure they would. I wanted to get them something besides just the slingshots. Let's add those to our purchases."

By the time they got through, they'd bought most everything on their lists. They had the books they'd talked about for the children, although Derrick wouldn't have minded buying one for himself. He liked to read.

They'd picked up a few more items for the families when Elise remembered to look for the ornaments his mother had requested. She found some pretty glass ones that Derrick was sure his mother would like. He'd have to go out and look for a tree to cut soon.

Elise also remembered to pick up some tissue paper and ribbon to wrap the presents in, and the yarn she wanted to give his mother for Christmas—plus the red and black yarn his mother wanted now. When they thought they had it all, Derrick went to get the wagon and took it to the first store to load the sewing machine. Then he came back for all the other things they'd purchased. The sun was setting when they headed back home.

❧

Elise couldn't remember when she'd enjoyed a day more. Derrick had a little-boy side she'd never seen until today. He'd had fun looking over all the toys for the boys and even those for the girls. He was very excited about the sewing machine he'd bought for his mother. But it was his admission that he'd once wanted to court her that had made the day most special for Elise.

He stopped the wagon at the house. "I'll bring everything in except the sewing machine. I'll keep that out in the barn until Christmas Eve. Then I'll bring it inside after she goes to sleep." He grinned. "I can't wait."

Elise laughed. His excitement was contagious. "Neither can I."

She helped him bring some of the packages in. Once they were inside, they were met by the wonderful aroma of vegetable soup simmering on the back of the stove.

"Oh, Mama, that smells delicious. I was wondering what to cook for supper," Elise said.

"I thought you might be getting hungry and be a little tired from your shopping trip." Frieda turned from stirring the soup. "How did it go? Were you able to get everything on our lists?"

"We were," Derrick answered his mother. "I'll let Elise tell you about it while I put up the wagon."

Elise took off Frieda's cloak and hung it on a hook in the pantry. "We got more than was on our list, but it was so much fun, Mama! Do you want me to show you everything now or wait until after supper?"

"After supper will be fine, dear. Now, just tell me what all you bought."

"Oh my, we bought a lot." She filled Frieda in on their purchases while she put the staples and other items away in the pantry. "I think they will like everything."

"I'm sure they will."

"How did you do today? Did you get finished with your blanket?"

Frieda popped the corn bread she'd mixed up into the oven. "Almost. I just have the last round to do and the fringe to put on it."

Elise hurried back into the pantry. "I almost forgot. We got the yarn you wanted."

"Wonderful!" Frieda took it and put it in her crochet bag.

Derrick came in the back door. "It's getting nippy out. If that soup tastes as good as it smells, it's going to be great, Mama."

"Thank you, son. I'm kind of out of practice, but I think it will be pretty good."

Elise set the table and ladled soup into the bowls before Derrick took them to the table. Once the corn bread was done, they all took their places and Derrick said the blessing.

"It sounds like our families will have a good Christmas," Frieda said. "I forgot to ask Elise what the preacher thought about your idea to give them a line of credit at the mercantile."

"He's more than willing to help me. I'll give him the money and he'll procure the line of credit for them. They won't ever know who paid for it."

"Sounds like all we have to do now is decide what we're making and when to deliver it all, then." Frieda said.

"We can get started trying some new recipes anytime you want, Mama," Elise said. "Some of the items can be made ahead, so we should be able to start our Christmas baking and candy making by the end of next week, don't you think?"

"I think that will be time enough to get it all done. Since Christmas falls on Monday, maybe we should distribute our gifts on Saturday?"

"I think that would be good. With Christmas Eve on Sunday this year, it will probably be better to make our deliveries earlier. We don't know what plans everyone might have. Besides, we'll be busy cooking and getting ready for Christmas ourselves," Elise suggested.

"We could even do it Friday. I'll get the things to Harold and Rachel by then so that they can get things to the Ballard and Hanson families well before Christmas," Derrick said.

"This is all so exciting. I think this is going to be the best Christmas we've had in a long time," his mother said.

"I know it's going to be the best one I've had in years," Derrick said. "Much as I like all we've planned to do, the best part for me is that I won't be alone."

Elise's heart went out to him, and she had a pretty good idea that his mother's was breaking at his honest statement. It must have been terribly lonely for him the past few years with no family around. Even if he ate a meal with Jed and Caroline, it wasn't the same as being part of all the preparations and having loved ones around.

It became even more important than ever that they have a good Christmas all together. She didn't know if she would be with Frieda and Derrick next year, for like it or not, she was going to have to go back to Denver. This day had meant too much to her—the man sitting across the table from her meant everything. Derrick had let her know that he'd once cared a great deal for her, but he didn't say that he still did. And because of that, she needed to go back to Denver. If she didn't leave soon, she'd never be able to hide how much she'd come to love Derrick. And just admitting that to herself filled her with guilt that she couldn't remember Carl's face anymore or even recall what their life had been like together—even less now that all of her waking thoughts seemed centered on Derrick and his admission that he'd once wanted to court her.

She had to leave. But she couldn't bring herself to do that before Christmas. She just couldn't. Not after hearing how much it meant to Derrick to have family around. And he and Frieda might do just fine by themselves, but she wouldn't. She couldn't force herself to leave until after the New Year. So until then—and especially for this Christmas—she was going to strive to do her part to make it the best she could for Derrick's sake, for his mother's sake, and even for her own.

&

The next day was Sunday, and the three of them were eager for Harold or Rachel to point out the Hanson and Ballard families to them. It would make it more fun to know who it was they were getting so excited about surprising.

Elise had been right about the Ballards. They were who she thought they were. Derrick was doubly pleased he'd bought the doll after seeing Anna. The doll even resembled the child with her blue eyes and blond hair. He was pretty sure the boys would like the presents they'd chosen, too.

As for the Hansons, their girls were beautiful young ladies who seemed very considerate of their parents. He hoped they liked the gifts they'd chosen for them. Their clothes were clean, if a little worn, and he felt good knowing they would be able to get something new or buy the dry goods to make something after Christmas. He was glad that he could help these families out, and he could hardly wait for Christmas to arrive.

That evening after supper, Elise and his mother decided to try out a new candy recipe. He volunteered to be their taste tester. He'd never had a praline before, but his mouth was watering even before the rich candy was cool enough to eat. It became an instant favorite along with the chocolate fudge thick with pecans that his mother always made.

"That's a definite winner. I'd say those should go out to everyone," he said after he finished the second one.

"Fudge and pralines—I think that's good for the candies, unless you want to make some fondant, Mama. You always have liked that," Elise said.

"We might. I do love a good fondant," his mother said. "We need to decide on the cookies or breads, too."

"Why don't you work on those tomorrow? I don't think I can test any more sweets tonight," Derrick said. Suddenly he wished he'd settled for only one praline. "I don't think I'm even up to hot cocoa tonight. But I can make some for you two."

Elise shook her head. "None for me, thank you. I've been nibbling here and there, too."

"I don't need any either, son. One of those candies goes a long way. Maybe we'd better put a warning on them."

⁊

During the next few days, Elise's guilt over her growing feelings for Derrick began to take away some of the joy she felt with their Christmas preparations. Finally, she decided she was going to have to start preparing Frieda for her eventual move back to Denver. If she told her, maybe, just maybe, she could start preparing herself.

They were trying out a new molasses cookie the next afternoon when Elise broached the subject with her mother-in-law. She waited until the cookies were out of the oven and they took an afternoon tea break to taste test them.

"Mama, after Christmas I'm going to have to make plans to go home to Denver," Elise said.

"Oh, Elise, I've been praying you would see that there's no need for you—"

"I can't stay here forever, Mama," Elise interrupted. "This is Derrick's home—and yours now—but it isn't mine." No matter how much she would like it to be.

"Elise, you know you're welcome to stay as long as you want."

Elise sighed heavily. "Mama, I know that. But. . .I—" She broke off the sentence and shook her head. It was time to be truthful with her mother-in-law. "I can't stay here. I'm beginning to care too much for Derrick, and I feel I'm being unfaithful to Carl's memory."

"Why, child, I know you loved Carl. But he's been gone over two years now. There's nothing wrong with you caring about Derrick the way you do. In fact, it's most likely because you and Carl had such a good marriage that you're able to fall in love with someone else and think of marriage again."

"Oh, Mama, I'm not sure. . ."

"Elise, dear, there's nothing I'd like better than to keep you in this family always. You are much too young to stay a widow forever. I know Carl would want you to go on with your life and be happy."

"I just don't know. I feel so bad that I can't even remember what Carl looked like without seeing his picture, Mama. And I feel guilty that it's Derrick who is in my thoughts so much."

Frieda reached out and patted her hand. "Elise, what you are going through is perfectly natural. You are young. You need a husband and a family to take care of."

"Maybe I do. But I don't know that Derrick wants that.

And even if he did, I don't know that it would be me he'd want it with. The longer I stay, the harder it's going to be for me to leave."

"Elise, dear, I can only tell you to take these concerns to the Lord. Ask Him to show you what to do. I don't want you to leave. I think you should stay right here. But I know you have to make that decision yourself. Please just pray about it. And I will do the same. The Lord will answer us in His time."

"I will pray, Mama." And she would. She needed the Lord's guidance as she'd never needed it before. She sent up a silent prayer just then, asking for Him to help her sort it all out and show her what to do, and—if it be His will—soon.

thirteen

As it turned colder, Derrick spent less time in the barn in the evening and took to spending time in the parlor reading the Good Book before going to bed. Hearing footsteps coming down the stairs one night, he looked up from reading and was surprised to see his mother coming back downstairs. Once she went up for the night, she rarely came back down.

"Mama, are you all right?" he asked as she shuffled into the room, wrapped in her warm robe.

"That depends." She seemed a woman on a mission as she crossed the room and took a seat on the sofa.

"What do you mean? Are you feeling poorly?"

"I'm feeling all right, I suppose." She sighed deeply, and he could see that something was bothering her. "I'm just sad."

"What are you sad about? Have I done anything to upset you?" He couldn't imagine what, but he did sometimes put his foot in his mouth.

"No, son. You haven't done anything. It's Elise—she's talking about going home to Denver again. She says she's going to make plans after Christmas."

Derrick felt as if a vise was squeezing his heart tighter and tighter until it took the breath right out of him. He could only manage to shake his head. When he could finally breathe again, he managed to get out, "No! She can't go, Mama. We can't let her."

"I don't see how we can stop her if she decides it's what she has to do, son."

"But I—*you* still need her here. You aren't up to—"

"Son, I'm doing better each day. But I don't want her to go any more than you do. Still, she feels she should be leaving. I've told her she's welcome—"

"So have I." Derrick got up and began pacing the room. Elise couldn't leave. He couldn't let her. "I've told her she can stay as long as she wants to. I guess she doesn't want to anymore."

"I don't think that's it, Derrick. I think she—"

"Have I done anything to upset her?"

"No, son, I don't believe you have. She's just. . ." His mother just sighed and shook her head.

Derrick needed some advice. It was time to open up to his mother. "Mama, what am I going to do? I love Elise. I don't want her to go!"

His mother nodded. "If that's the case—and I suspected it might be—why haven't you told Elise how you feel, Derrick?"

He dropped back down into his chair. "Mama, I've loved Elise for years. I've cared for her since even before Carl started courting her."

"Did she know?"

"No, not then." Derrick shook his head. "Carl started wooing her and. . . Well, when she accepted his proposal of marriage, I thought my heart would surely break. That's why I left Colorado in the first place."

"I see. I never knew, although I did wonder about it."

"There was no point in telling you, Mama. It would only have upset you. But Carl knew how I felt about Elise before he ever decided to try to court her, and I can tell you now that I was unhappy with my brother for a good long time. Still, it really was my fault. I should have acted before he had a chance to."

"I see."

He wasn't sure she did. Even he didn't know why he hadn't pursued Elise before Carl did. He continued explaining, "Once they were married, I knew I couldn't stay in Denver and watch them start a life together. It was just too hard for me. So I began a new one here."

His mother nodded. "Now I understand why you left and moved here. But Carl has passed away, and Elise has come back into your life."

Derrick nodded and put his head in his hands. "I don't know what to do, Mama. I don't want to lose her again. I did let her know that I'd wanted to court her but that Carl beat me to the asking. I felt I had to let her know." He shook his head. "But I still don't know if she'll ever see me as anything but Carl's brother."

"Son, you did the right thing by leaving Denver and coming to New Mexico Territory—feeling about Elise the way you did. And Elise made your brother very happy. But that was then. Carl is gone, and now Elise is alone. It could be all in God's plan for you and Elise to be together now. After all, she had plenty of suitors at our door in Denver before we came down here. But none of them interested her. And none of them had her blushing at their nearness or at their teasing like she does around you, Derrick."

Derrick felt a glimmer of hope begin to grow at his mother's words. He had noticed that there were times when Elise's face flushed with color when they were together. "You think she might care?"

"I believe so. But, Derrick, if you don't want her going back to Denver, you need to take action. Pray on it and let the Lord lead you to find the way to let her know how you feel."

It was what Derrick wanted to do with all his heart, and

yet. . . What if Elise didn't return his feelings? What if he could never measure up to his brother? But his mother was right—it was time he took it all to the Lord. "I'll do that, Mama. It's for sure I don't know what to do on my own."

"He'll guide you. Just be still and listen," his mother said. "I'm going up to bed now. I'll be praying for the Lord to show you what to do, too, Derrick."

"Thank you, Mama. Sleep well."

She kissed his cheek on the way out the door. Derrick felt better after telling her how he felt about Elise, but still, the fact that Elise was thinking about going back to Denver gave him a heavy heart. He didn't want to lose her again.

Derrick went back to his Bible and tried to take up where he'd left off. But thoughts of Elise kept filling his mind. Finally, he bowed his head and began to whisper, "Dear Lord, I need You to help me. Elise is talking about leaving once more. Father, You know I don't want that. You know I love her. Yet I'm afraid to let her know how I feel. I lost her to my brother before—and I could always use that as an excuse for my heartache—but deep down, I know that it was my own inaction that gave Carl the opportunity to win her heart. I can't blame him forever. And it could be that even with Carl gone now, Elise might not ever feel the same about me as I do her." He sighed and rubbed his temple before continuing to open up his heart. "I'm afraid to find out how she feels about me—and I'm afraid not to. Lord, please let me know what to do. Family relationships count on me doing the right thing. While I pray it's Your will that Elise become my wife, I want to do what truly is *Your* will. Please guide me in this, Lord. In Jesus' name I pray. Amen."

❧

Elise slept fitfully that night. She did feel better that Frieda knew how she felt about Derrick, but at the same time, she still didn't know what to do about it all. It wasn't as if she could just walk up to him and tell him she loved him.

No, all she could do was pray that if he cared about her, he would let her know soon. She didn't want to hurt the good relationship they had as in-laws. She wanted to be able to see Frieda again. Hopefully she could talk her into spending part of the year here and part of the year in Denver with her. Yet Elise wasn't sure her mother-in-law was up to that kind of upheaval in her life. Coming down here had taken its toll. Going back and forth—well, that just might be too much for her.

She tried to shake off her forlornness as she came downstairs. Christmas was coming, and they had a lot to do. She'd have to think about it all later. She was surprised to find her mother-in-law already there, standing at the range, making breakfast. "My, you're up early, Mama."

"I just woke up with a hankering for pancakes, dear. I thought I'd see if I still knew how to make them."

Elise looked at the golden rounds on the griddle. "It certainly looks as if you do. Those look perfect. I love your pancakes!"

"I'm glad to hear it." Frieda looked out the window. "I see Derrick coming this way. Will you get the butter and maple syrup out?"

"Certainly." Elise could feel her face flush at the mere mention of Derrick's name, and she knew it was because Frieda was now aware of how Elise felt about her younger son. But Elise trusted that her mother-in-law hadn't told him how she felt, and she didn't mention anything about it now. Frieda had never been one to meddle in her children's affairs of the heart. Elise knew that from experience.

"Good morning!" Derrick said as he entered the kitchen

and smiled at her. "It's a beautiful day out. But it's cold. It's feeling a little like Christmas."

Elise's heart was hammering against her ribs as Derrick's gaze never left her face. She forced herself to respond to his comment about the weather. "Do you think it might snow for Christmas?"

"It's always a possibility. We had a white Christmas year before last." Finally, Derrick broke eye contact and hung his coat on the hook, then went to the stove to warm his hands. "Mmm, Mama, those pancakes smell delicious!"

Frieda put the last of the pancakes on the platter and handed it to him. "I hope they are. Take these to the table, please."

She then took the bacon out of the warmer and brought it to the table. "This should get us going. We have a lot to do today."

"I thought I'd go scout out a tree—unless you need me here to help," Derrick said as he forked a couple of pancakes onto his plate, spread them with butter, and poured syrup over them.

"I think we can handle the baking today. You go on and look for a tree," Frieda said as she took her seat. "Will you cut it already?"

"I might. Depends on how far I have to go to find one. I can put it in a bucket of water until we're ready for it next week. But if it's nearby, I'll probably just wait until closer to Christmas."

"I am so excited about starting our family tradition here," Frieda said. "I've missed it so much."

Elise thought back to the past several years and realized they'd done well to celebrate Christmas at all. The first year after Carl died was a bad one. And last year wasn't much better, but she found herself truly looking forward to this year. She'd think about next year. . .well, next year. "I wish I'd known, Mama. We could have done more in Colorado."

"I know. But after Papa passed away and then Carl. . .it took awhile to get over all that heartache."

"I should have come up there. I'm sorry, Mama and Elise," Derrick said. "I shouldn't have let you two go through that heartache alone. Instead, I stayed here and we were all miserable."

"That is the past, son. We must all let go of it and look forward to the future. We have some cherished—and some fading—memories. But our loved ones are in a better place now, and we must get on with life."

Elise had a feeling her mother-in-law was trying to get her to see that she should treasure her memories of Carl but not worry that they were not as clear as they once were. And that she should feel free to love again. If so, it was what Elise wanted to hear. But even if she could get past the guilt she felt because Derrick had taken up a bigger chunk of her heart than Carl's memory held, she still didn't really know how he felt about her now.

❧

When Derrick came in later in the day, it was to find a whole table full of molasses cookies. "I feel like a kid again just waiting for Mama to get busy so I can grab a cookie and run outside. Carl and I both used to do that." He sniffed appreciatively. "These smell just like I remember them."

His mother laughed. "I knew what you and Carl were up to. But don't you dare snitch one of those. That's the first full batch of cookies we've made. I think we have about twelve dozen, don't we, Elise?"

"Yes. At least I hope so." Elise turned from the stew she was stirring. "We have eleven families, besides us, that we're making goodies for—including the Hansons and the Ballards."

"I didn't realize I'd made so much work for you two. We can make the list shorter."

"And hurt a neighbor's feelings? No, we don't want to do that," his mother said.

"We can handle it. Besides, we're going to put you to work chopping pecans tonight, Derrick. You aren't going to get out of all the work," Elise said in a teasing tone.

"I'll be glad to help. I can't let you girls have all the fun," Derrick bantered back. "Guess what?" he asked while he washed his hands at the sink. "I found a tree. It's beautiful, and it's just over the way past the Jonathan apple trees. Since it's so close, I'll wait until you're ready to put it up to cut it."

She and Frieda hadn't bothered with a tree the past few years, and Elise was excited at the prospect of putting one up. She could see that Mama was, too. "When do you think we should put it up?"

"We used to always put it up on Christmas Eve. But since it's on Sunday this year, and we'll be taking our Christmas baskets out on Saturday, why don't we put it up on Friday?" Frieda said.

"The sooner the better as far as I'm concerned," Elise said as she ladled the stew into bowls.

"I have to admit I'm excited about it going up, too. I haven't had a Christmas tree since I left home." Derrick took the full bowls to the kitchen table.

"We're all agreed, then. We'll put it up on Friday night. We'd better start popping some corn soon. It won't hurt to start stringing it now," Elise said when she and Frieda joined him at the table.

"I'll start popping anytime you say," Derrick said. "I can

chop nuts and string popcorn at night."

"That's good, because we're going to keep you busy doing just that," his mother said.

Derrick felt blessed beyond measure that he had his mother and Elise to spend this Christmas with. He didn't know what the future held for him and Elise, but he'd been busy talking to the Lord about it. Now as he said the blessing, he thanked the Lord for all they had and were about to eat, knowing that the Lord also heard the prayer he wasn't voicing at the moment—the one he'd been praying about off and on all day. And Derrick had faith that the Lord would give him an answer. . .in His time.

fourteen

The next few days were very busy with cookie baking. They were saving the candy making until the next week. On Saturday morning, they sent Derrick into town for more cookie tins and baskets to place their gifts in.

As the day went on, Elise was a little concerned that her mother-in-law didn't seem as energetic as she had the past few days. But nothing would satisfy Frieda but to be in the kitchen helping.

"Mama, I forgot to ask about the blanket for little Jonathan. Have you been able to finish it?"

"I have. And I'm eager to get it to him. Maybe I'll take it in tomorrow and give it to them at church—if they're there. Or we can wait and I can wrap it up as a Christmas present to add to the basket we're taking them."

"Either way would work."

"I sure would like to see that baby. I'm glad we've been so busy, though. Otherwise, I'd have missed him something terrible."

"I'm sorry Carl and I couldn't make you a grandmother, Mama."

"Oh, I didn't mean for you to feel bad about that, Elise. I know how badly you wanted a child."

The squeak of wagon wheels alerted them to Derrick's arrival back from town just then. Elise hurried out to help him bring in the baskets and tins.

"I'm glad I went today. They were getting low on these,"

Derrick said, bringing in the last of the baskets. "But I have some news. Guess what?"

"What is it? What's going on in town?"

"I ran into Jed and Caroline and little Jonathan! They were in town to pick up Caroline's parents who've come for Christmas. They're very nice people, and they couldn't wait to get that baby in their arms."

"Oh, I'm glad they're here! How are Caroline and the baby?" his mother asked.

"Caroline was glowing with health, and the baby has filled out and put on some weight from when we saw him last. Caroline says he's growing like a little weed."

"Oh, I would so like to see him," Frieda said.

"You'll get to tomorrow. They all plan on being at church."

"Wonderful! I'm still not sure when to give them the layette I made, but I'll figure it out before tomorrow. I'm anxious to meet Caroline's family."

Elise was pleased that the anticipation of seeing baby Jonathan again seemed to perk her mother-in-law up for the rest of the day.

❧

Excitement over seeing baby Jonathan had Derrick's mother up early, and she was ready long before they needed to leave for church.

"Are you going to give the baby present to them today, Mama?" Elise asked as they ate a breakfast of biscuits and gravy.

"I think I'll wait and give it to them for Christmas. I don't want to take away from their excitement about having her family here and bringing the baby to church. I can't wait to see them all, though."

Derrick took the stones he'd been warming out to the

wagon just before they got ready to leave. When they took off, Derrick was glad that the day wasn't quite as cold as the last few had been. Otherwise, he might have had to give Elise her Christmas present early. That cloak of hers wasn't meant for winter weather.

They arrived at church just about the time Jed pulled up with Caroline, the baby, and her parents. After introductions were made, they all hurried inside to keep the baby out of the cool weather.

The Barristers and Caroline's parents, Mr. and Mrs. Walton, sat on the same pew with them, and it didn't take long for little Jonathan to travel from one set of arms to another until he wound up in Derrick's mother's arms. The look on her face was priceless. And there was no mistaking the longing in Elise's eyes as she took her own turn holding the baby. Derrick had a feeling that she wanted a family of her own just as badly as he did. When she looked over and her glance met his, he wondered if she had any inkling at all of how much he wanted her for his wife.

Derrick's heart hammered in his chest at the thought that it might be possible they both wanted the very same thing. Just as the service began, he sent up a silent prayer that the Lord would show them that they did.

When the service was over, Jed and Caroline asked if they would join them for dinner at the hotel. Derrick readily agreed. His mother and Elise could use a break from all the cooking they were doing.

They were seated at a round table, but the three men sat close so they could talk. Somehow, though, Elise ended up sitting next to Derrick, with his mother next to her. Caroline's dad sat between him and Jed, with Caroline on Jed's other side and her mother next to her. Mrs. Walton and Derrick's mother took turns holding the baby during the meal.

Caroline and Jed had already told her parents how much Derrick and his family had done for them, and her parents thanked them over and over for being there for their daughter and son-in-law. By the end of the meal, they all felt like family. When they got back home, Derrick was pleased that his mother seemed very happy, if a little tired.

Elise must have noticed, too, because she put on the tea-kettle and then turned to his mother, who'd sat down at the table. "Mama, why don't we wait until tomorrow to finish our baking and start the candy making? I'm sure we have time to get it all done, and you've been on your feet an awful lot this week."

"I am a little tired. But, oh, wasn't it good to see the Barristers? And that baby is so adorable! I really like Caroline's parents, too."

"Her papa said they were thinking of moving out here," Derrick said. "Caroline is an only child, and they want little Jonathan to grow up knowing his grandparents."

"I can certainly understand that," his mother said. "I hope they do make the move here. It's good for families to live close to each other."

⁊♠

The next morning, Elise had breakfast on the table before Frieda came downstairs. It seemed to Derrick that his mother was moving a little slower than usual. "Mama, are you feeling all right this morning?"

Frieda sat down at the table. "I'm feeling a little weak for some reason."

"Most probably because you did too much this last week," Elise said. "I was afraid I was letting you overdo things."

"It's not your fault, Elise, dear. All this was my idea, remember?"

"Well, I don't want you wearing yourself out right before Christmas. I know you had your heart set on doing a lot, but it's important to us that you don't overdo. I'd like to do the rest of the baking and candy making—with you supervising, of course—if it's all right with you."

Derrick's heart warmed at the way Elise still tried to make his mother feel needed, even though he was sure she knew quite well what needed to be done.

"I can't let you do it all, Elise."

"Mama, I can help Elise when I get through doing all my chores."

"Are you sure?"

"Of course I am. We'll do fine—as long as you supervise."

His mother sighed and nodded. "All right, then, I'll let you two do all the standing. I can sit here and crochet or string popcorn. I'm sorry I won't be doing my share—with this being my idea and all."

"Mama, it may have been your idea, but Derrick and I are both as excited about it as you are," Elise said, bringing a plate of sausage and eggs to the table. "You eat and rest and get your strength back. The last thing we want is for you to have a relapse of the pneumonia."

"I don't think that's what this is. I'm not coughing and my chest isn't hurting. It's just that my legs are giving me a little trouble, that's all. I'm sure I'll feel better in a day or two."

"Maybe, if you rest. And Elise and I are going to make sure you do," Derrick said as he helped himself to a couple of eggs and some sausage. "I'll get through with the chores as soon as I can and be in to help."

"Thank you, son."

Derrick was looking forward to helping Elise. She was so competent she rarely needed help at all, but with Mama feeling poorly again, Elise wouldn't have much choice in accepting his help. When he came in that afternoon, however, Elise already had several batches of fudge made.

"Mmm, I love coming in the house—especially the last few days. It always smells so good," he said. "Where's Mama?"

"I convinced her to take a nap. I really don't want her getting sick again, but she just doesn't seem to have the energy she did last week."

"Has she been sleeping long?" He took off his coat and hung it on a hook beside the back door.

Elise shook her head. "No, she went up not long before you came in. I told her I'd call her when supper was ready."

"What can I do to help?"

"Why don't you wrap up some of this fudge? The tissue paper is there on the table. You can wrap it like a present or pull the sides up and tie it with ribbon—however you want to do it."

"Uh, all right." Derrick had never been great at wrapping things, but he was willing to try. He washed his hands and went over to the table, where pans of candy were cooled and waiting to be cut.

"How big do you want the pieces to be?"

"Oh, cut them in about two-inch squares. I think that should be about right."

He could do that. Derrick sliced the fudge into nice, neat pieces. But it was when he started wrapping them that he ran into problems. "Uh, Elise?"

She looked up from pouring another pan of fudge. "Yes?"

"I really don't know how to wrap candy—or much of anything else for that matter."

She chuckled and put the empty pot into the sink. "I'll help."

It took several tries before they decided that stacking several pieces of fudge in the middle of the tissue paper and then pulling up all the sides and tying the package with a ribbon worked best and was the easiest way to do it.

"I think I've got it now," Derrick said, looking down at the top of Elise's head while she tied a ribbon around the gathered-up paper he was holding.

She smiled up at him. "Are you sure?"

"I think so." He'd been tempted to tell her no, just so she would stay and help him—not that he needed the help—as he loved the smell of her hair and the nearness of her. He wanted nothing more right at that moment than to claim her lips in a kiss. But she finished the bow and moved away before he could turn his thoughts into action.

"Good. I need to check on the roast I have in the oven for supper. Tonight I'm going to try my hand at making some popcorn balls."

"Now that's something I can help with. Carl and I used to help Mama make them."

"I'm glad to hear it. I can use all the help you want to give. I've never made them before."

Derrick was more than glad to help her. His kitchen had turned into his favorite room in the house, because it was where Elise could most often be found. For the next half hour, they worked together getting the fudge wrapped, and then Derrick set the table while Elise finished up supper.

He was just about to go up and check on his mother when she came through the door.

"There you are! How are you feeling, Mama?"

"A tad better, I think. I heard some laughter down here earlier. You two sounded like you were having a good time."

"I couldn't figure out how to wrap the fudge," Derrick

explained. "And then after I thought I knew what to do, Elise had to show me how to make a bow."

His mother looked at the tissue-wrapped candy. "The packages look quite nice to me. They don't have to be perfect."

After supper, Derrick took it on himself to pop the popcorn while Elise cleaned up the supper dishes. He popped two large pans full. Then he turned to his mother. "Okay, it's just the syrup that we add to the corn, right, Mama?"

"No, it's more than that, son. You need to combine one cup of sugar, a cup of syrup, one tablespoon of vinegar, and a teaspoon of salt together and cook that mixture to hardball stage."

"I thought you knew how to do this," Elise teased.

Derrick laughed and looked at her. "Uh. . .I guess Carl and I just got to mix it all together."

"That's what you did, all right," his mother said.

Elise got out a pan and mixed all the ingredients together and put them on to boil. "Once it reaches hardball, Mama, then what do we do?"

"You remove it from the heat and add a tablespoon of butter to it. Oh yes, Derrick, salt the popcorn, too. Next you mix it all together until all the kernels are coated with the syrup. Then you quickly form the coated popcorn into about three-inch balls."

As soon as the mixture was ready, Derrick helped Elise pour it over the popped corn. It wasn't but a minute before they were all laughing as he and Elise tried forming the balls. "I forgot how sticky they are, Mama. Why didn't you remind me that we needed to butter our hands?"

"I couldn't resist seeing the looks on your faces when you tried to get the mixture into a ball and off your hands. I haven't laughed like this in a long time."

"Well, I'm glad you're having such a good time." Derrick grinned at her while he and Elise quickly washed their hands and started over. This time they managed to form the sticky popcorn into nice round balls. Derrick knew that he and Carl had never had quite this much fun as kids. He would cherish the memory always, and he knew he would never eat another popcorn ball without thinking about Elise.

❧

The next few days and evenings were full of fun and work. But by Thursday night, they had everything made and wrapped to be put in boxes or baskets the next day. On Friday, Derrick was going to take the Hansons' and Ballards' presents—along with the money for the line of credit for them—to Harold and Rachel's place. Then he would come back to cut the Christmas tree so they could put it up that evening. He couldn't wait to see how the house looked once they'd put on the glass ornaments and the garland of popcorn they'd all taken a turn at stringing. It was going to be the best Christmas he'd ever had, and he prayed it wouldn't be the last with Elise.

fifteen

When Elise went down to start breakfast Friday morning, it was with mixed feelings. She was more excited about their Christmas plans than she'd ever been, but it would soon be over, and once it was, she was going to have to make plans to go home.

The last few days had been wonderful and full of fun, working with Derrick to finish all the Christmas goodies they planned to give out. She would have memories that were bound to be both wonderful and bittersweet throughout the coming years. But Elise just could not continue to stay here any longer only as Carl's widow. She wanted to be a living part of this family—not part of it only because she'd been married to Frieda's son and Derrick's brother.

After spending so much time with Derrick, she was fully aware that she was head over heels in love with him. She could not continue to live in his home, taking care of it and caring about him more each day, without wanting to be his wife. There. She'd admitted it—if only to herself. No. It wasn't just to herself. The Lord knew how she felt.

There'd been a few times in the last few months, and particularly the last few days, when she thought Derrick might care about her in the same way—especially after he'd told her he'd once wanted to court her. But she didn't know if he really did or if it was just wishful thinking on her part. All she did know was that it was going to hurt badly enough to leave here in the next few weeks. If she stayed and fell even deeper in love with him and he didn't return her feelings, it would only create more heartache in the long run. Better to go through it now.

But since Christmas was upon them, Elise pushed sad thoughts away as she forked up the bacon she was frying. She was determined to enjoy the next few days. Memories of them might well be all she had in the coming years.

Derrick entered the kitchen just as his mother came in from upstairs. "Good morning, Mama and Elise. Can you believe it? I'm almost sad because all of the cooking is done."

"Oh, not all of it, son. We still have Christmas dinner to look forward to. How is that turkey doing out in the pen?"

"It's getting fatter by the day." Derrick chuckled. "Are you two ready to decorate the tree tonight?"

"I think so." Elise smiled as she brought the food to the table. "Are we going to put it in the parlor?"

"You know, we spend so much time in the kitchen, I wouldn't mind putting it right here. But wherever you two want it is fine with me. I'll be bringing it up when I get back from town."

❧

After supper, Derrick brought the tree in and set it up in front of the window by the kitchen table. They hung the popcorn garland and then the glass ornaments that Elise had picked out in town. Feeling it needed a bit more color, they strung cranberries while they drank Derrick's hot cocoa. When they put that garland up, they all agreed it was just what the tree needed.

"No matter how many trees I put up in this house, I'll always remember this first one," Derrick said.

"It's lovely," Elise said, standing across the room to take a good look. "I'll always remember it, too."

Later that evening, Elise brought down the prettily wrapped

presents she'd bought for Derrick and his mother, only to find several other packages already under the tree, two of them with her name on them. She suddenly felt like a child again, and the hope of the season flooded her. She placed her packages under the tree and sent up a silent prayer, finally asking the Lord outright to let her know soon how Derrick felt about her. And that—if it be His will—she would never have to go back to Denver to stay.

&

"I think there's going to be a weather change," Derrick's mother said around noon the next day when they were about to eat dinner. "I can feel it in my bones. They're kind of achy."

"It's a mite colder outside now than it was this morning," Derrick said. He'd just come in from doing some chores and was warming his hands over the range.

"Maybe I ought not to go with you two to deliver the baskets this afternoon. All that going in and out in the cold might not be the best thing for me now that I'm feeling better. I sure don't want to feel poorly tomorrow and have to miss church."

"Mama, I hate for you to miss out on the fun since all this was your idea," Derrick said. "I know you've been looking forward to it, but I certainly don't want you to chance getting sick again right now. And I know you want to go to church tomorrow, especially since it's Christmas Eve."

"I hate not to go with you two, but I think you're right. You and Elise can deliver it all. I'm just glad to know we've started the tradition back up. I do want to go to church tomorrow, and I'm afraid that all the up and down, getting in and out of the wagon, and into one house and then another might be a bit tiresome. You two can tell me all about it when you get home."

"I do so hate that you won't be with us, Mama, but I'll try to remember every last detail to share with you when we get back," Elise promised as she fixed their plates and brought them to the table. "I'll put on a pot of soup before we leave, and when we return we can tell you all about our visits over supper."

"I'll have the table set and ready. I can do that much at least," Frieda said. "I also think I'll keep the present for the Barristers here and take it to them tomorrow. But you can take them the cookies and candy."

"I think that's a good idea. That way at least you'll get the joy of giving the baby's gift to them in person," Elise said.

While Elise cleaned up the kitchen and put on the vegetable soup for supper, Derrick began loading the wagon with the baskets they were giving out.

"We can take off whenever you're ready, Elise," he said as he came in from loading the last of the baskets. "Dress as warmly as you can. It's getting colder out."

"Please wear my cloak, Elise, dear. I don't want you getting sick."

"I will borrow it, since you aren't going. I'm going to have to—" Elise suddenly shook her head and turned to go upstairs. "It won't take me long to change."

"Take your time," Derrick said. "I'll heat a rock for your feet." He pulled out one of the rocks they kept in the fire box just for that reason and stuck it inside the range.

Elise had no more than left the kitchen when his mother motioned for him to come close. "Son, if you're going to do anything to stop Elise from going back to Denver, you'd better be planning on doing it soon," she whispered.

Derrick only nodded and turned away. He knew full well he was running out of time. He took the rock from the range and wrapped it in a towel just as Elise came back downstairs. She looked lovely in a green and white striped dress that seemed very Christmassy.

"Oh, how nice you look, Elise," his mother said. "I do feel I've let the two of you down this week. I'm sorry."

"You haven't let us down at all, Mama," Elise said, kissing her on the cheek. "We do wish you were up to coming with us, but better that you're up to going to church tomorrow and enjoying Christmas Day with us."

"Yes, well, I pray you two will have a wonderful time this afternoon."

"Keep an eye on that soup for us, Mama. We'll be back before you know it." Derrick helped Elise slip into his mother's cloak, then they headed out the door.

Outside, Derrick assisted Elise into the wagon, then went around and climbed up on the other side. He looked at the heavy sky. "I think it may snow before Christmas gets here."

"Do you really?" Elise asked, her eyes shining like a child's.

"I do." Derrick flipped the reins and they took off. "Perhaps I can pull out the sleigh."

"You have a sleigh? I haven't ridden in one in years!"

"I do. Actually, it's one more thing that came with this place. I've only had it out a time or two, but it's quite fun." He hoped he'd have a chance to take her for a ride.

As they traveled down the road, Elise turned quiet, watching the scenery, and Derrick sent up one silent prayer after another. He prayed he would have the courage to tell her how much he loved her before this night was over. He prayed that he could convince her not to go back to Denver. He wasn't sure how he was going to go about it exactly, but he had faith that the Lord was going to guide him. He couldn't put it off any longer. If he did, he might lose Elise forever.

Elise was sorry that Frieda couldn't make the trip, but she couldn't say she was disappointed to have this time with Derrick alone. She enjoyed stopping at each neighbor's home and handing out the baskets of baked goods and candies.

At the Millers', the children couldn't wait to try the fudge. And at the Sanders', it was the popcorn balls that garnered the most attention. Without fail, all of Derrick's neighbors were pleased by his gifts to them.

"What a good idea this is. I'd like to do something like this next year," Maude Sanders said when Derrick explained that it was his mother's idea to carry on a family tradition. "I seem to remember my grandparents giving out different kinds of breads at Christmastime. It would be good to get the children involved in something like this."

Derrick exchanged a glance with Elise and chuckled. "I guarantee they'll have a good time. But it isn't just for children. Adults can have just as good a time working together."

Elise could feel the color rise into her cheeks. There was something in Derrick's expression—as his gaze captured hers— that had her heart fluttering in her chest. She didn't quite know what it was, but it had her feeling a bit. . .breathless.

As the afternoon wore on, they were welcomed into each house and offered coffee or tea or hot cocoa. They didn't stay long anywhere, but it was enough time to give her several good stories to tell to Mama when they got back to the house.

It was at the Barristers' where they stayed the longest time, however. Baby Jonathan was wide awake, and Elise couldn't resist holding him awhile. Derrick didn't seem to be in any hurry, as he, Jed, and Caroline's father talked about the weather and farming in this part of the country.

Elise looked down at the baby in her arms. He was

adorable. "Oh, Caroline, he's grown just in a week."

"I know. He's filling out and changing so much. It seems there's something new about him each day. I wish Frieda could have come."

"She's been a bit tired this past week, and we all thought it might be best if she stayed in today so that she would feel like going to church tomorrow."

"Oh no, we don't want her getting sick again. I'm glad she'll be at church tomorrow. At least we'll get to see her then," Caroline said.

"Giving out baskets to the neighbors was actually her idea," Elise said. "It was a family tradition that Derrick plans on continuing here."

"This is so nice," Caroline's mother said as she looked into the basket and saw all the goodies they'd made. "We've managed to make a few sweets, but Jonathan takes up a lot of our time. I'll tell her tomorrow, of course, but please let Mrs. Morgan know how thankful we are for all of this."

"I will," Elise promised.

By the time they left the Barristers', it was almost suppertime. This was their last stop, so they headed for home.

Much as she hated the time alone to end, Elise loved seeing the light pouring out of Derrick's windows. The house looked warm and welcoming. Derrick dropped her off at the back door and then went on to the barn.

His mother must have been listening for them, because she was ladling up steaming bowls of soup when Elise came inside.

"It's getting colder out there, Mama! Derrick will be here as soon as he feeds the horse and puts the wagon up," she said, taking off the cloak and hanging it on its customary hook. She hurried across the room. "Here, let me help you."

"Just take these over to the table, dear." Frieda handed her a bowl. "This should warm you both up. How did it go?"

"Oh, Mama, everyone was so appreciative, and they thought your tradition was just wonderful. I think several of the women will try to do something similar next year."

Frieda nodded and smiled. "Good. That's what I hoped would happen. Swapping small gifts and visiting helps to bring neighbors closer together." She took the corn bread she'd made out of the warmer just as Derrick came inside.

"Mmm, that smells delicious!"

"It does," his mother replied. "And I have to admit I'm a bit hungry. I've smelled it all afternoon. You and Elise can tell me all about the afternoon right after you say the blessing, son."

⋅❧⋅

Derrick did say the blessing, but he added a silent prayer of his own. *Dear Lord, please help me to tell Elise how I feel about her tonight. I've been on the verge of telling her all day, but I'm running out of time and I need to let her know how I feel. Please give me the words to say, and, Father, please let her feel the same way. In Jesus' name I pray. Amen.*

"Elise tells me that everyone liked our gifts. Did you get to see Caroline and the baby and Jed?"

"We did. I mostly visited with Jed and his father-in-law, while Elise visited with Caroline and her mother. She can tell you about the baby."

"I got to hold Jonathan. Oh, Mama, he's growing so! Caroline was disappointed that you weren't able to come, but she's looking forward to showing him off to you tomorrow."

"I can't wait to see him. Have her parents said if they have decided to stay?"

"Well, her father is looking at property in the area," Derrick said. "That's a good signal that they might be. They really didn't say outright, though."

"Oh, I hope they do. I know that will mean a lot to Caroline and Jed, and her parents, too, for them all to have family close."

After supper, Derrick helped Elise clean up the kitchen, and they both entertained his mother with stories about the Miller and Sanders children and how excited they were about the baskets.

"Oh, and, Mama, Caroline and her mother were so happy to have the cookies and candy," Elise said. "With taking care of Jonathan, they haven't been able to do all the cooking they would have liked to do for Christmas."

"Well, I'm glad everyone liked our gifts. It makes it all worthwhile—although the two of you did most of the work."

"It was your idea, Mama," Derrick said. "I wouldn't have attempted it otherwise. And it's for certain we'd never have gotten those popcorn balls made without you. They were quite a hit with the children especially."

"Well now, that is quite true. I'm not sure what you would have had if you'd just mixed that syrup in with the popcorn," his mother said.

"A gooey mess, most probably." Derrick laughed and made a face.

"It was quite fun, though," Elise added.

His mother laughed just thinking about it again.

"Would either of you like a cup of cocoa?" Derrick asked.

"I was just waiting for you to make it. Then I'm going up. I'm getting sleepy," his mother said.

While Derrick made the tasty drink, he tried to think of ways to talk to Elise after his mother went upstairs. Elise usually went up at the same time, but Derrick was determined to talk to her—to tell her how he felt about her. He had to.

As he stirred the ingredients together, he sent up a silent plea. *I know I should have brought it up while we were out today, Lord. But please give me the courage to talk to her tonight. I know that even if she says she could never love me, You will see me through. I finally realize that's exactly what You did when I let my brother win her heart. You saw me through the pain then, and even though I couldn't see it at the time, I see it now. So please just guide me, help me find the right words, and if my heart is broken once more, I'm trusting in You to see me through.*

"Derrick, son! Are you scorching our cocoa?"

He hurriedly took the pot off the stove. "No, I think it's all right, Mama, but I'm glad you got my attention."

"You must have been woolgathering," his mother said with a chuckle.

"Mmm," Derrick said noncommittally. No, what he'd been doing was much more important than daydreaming—much more important.

sixteen

Elise helped him take the cups of the frothy drink to the table. Derrick tried to keep his mind on the conversation as his mother and Elise talked over the day again and pondered whether the Ballards and the Hansons were going to like their gifts. But it wasn't easy to do. All he really wanted was for his dear mother to retire for the night and for him to find some way to talk to Elise before she followed his mother up.

They seemed to linger over the steaming cups of cocoa, but finally his mother yawned and said, "I guess it's time I went to bed. I'll help you clean up first, though, Elise."

Suddenly Derrick had his opening. As his mother stood up and picked up her cup to take it to the sink, Derrick quickly took it from her. "I'll put this up, Mama. And I'll help Elise clean up. You go on to bed."

He looked at her intently, hoping she would read his mind as well as she'd seemed to when he was a child.

"Well, all right, son. I'll see you two tomorrow. Be sure not to let me oversleep."

Derrick placed a kiss on her delicate cheek. "We won't. Good night."

Elise turned from the sink she was filling with water. "Good night, Mama. I hope you sleep well."

Derrick brought his and his mother's cups to the sink, turning to make sure she'd left the room. "Uh. . .Elise, I—"

"Look, Derrick!" Elise interrupted him as she peered out the window. "I think I just saw a snowflake."

Derrick looked over her shoulder. "It wouldn't surprise me if we have snow on the ground tomorrow," he said.

"Really?" Elise asked, her eyes shining bright as she turned to him.

They were standing so close she was near to being in his arms. All he would have to do was slide them around her. He looked into her eyes, and something in her expression held his gaze. His heart was hammering hard against his chest. "It's possible," he said to her.

Elise never broke eye contact as she smiled at him, and Derrick felt a flash of hope. He reminded himself that with God all things truly were possible. It was time to step out in faith. He slid his arms around Elise and looked deep into her eyes.

"Elise, I don't want one more day to pass without telling you. . .that. . .I love you." Her eyes widened, and if anything, her smile grew larger, giving him the courage to go on. "I have loved you for years. Do you think you could ever feel the same way about me?"

"Oh, Derrick. . ." She shook her head.

His heart seemed to stop beating as he waited for her to continue. He could see the tears that gathered in her eyes, and he held his breath, waiting for her to break his heart once more.

Elise reached up to touch his cheek. "I already *do* feel the same way about you. I've been in love with you for months now, and I was afraid—"

Derrick didn't let her finish the sentence. His lips claimed hers in a kiss that told her just how long he'd waited to hear her words. Hoping he'd convinced her of how much he cared, he lifted his lips from hers and looked deep into her eyes. "I've dreamed of this moment for so long, Elise."

She smiled at him. "Now might be the time to tell you that you *were* too slow back then. Happy as I was with Carl, and as much as I came to love him, there was a time when it was *you* I was hoping would court me. I've been hoping you still felt the same ever since you told me you'd wanted to do just that."

"I never stopped caring about you, Elise. The love I felt for you has only grown over time." Derrick paused and took a deep breath before continuing. "Will you marry me. . .now, before the year is out? I can think of nothing I'd like more than to start the new year with you as my wife. That's all I want for Christmas—for us to be married."

"Oh yes, Derrick, I will marry you, before the end of the year, if we can get the preacher to do it that soon."

He claimed her lips in another kiss that very effectively promised their love to each other. It was only the sound of a loud whoop from outside the kitchen that broke them apart.

"Mama?" Elise said. They turned to find Frieda barreling into the room, breathing hard.

"Mama, are you all right?" Derrick hurriedly seated her at the table while Elise filled a glass with water. "Maybe I should go for the doctor?"

"No!" his mother finally said. "There's no need for the doctor," she assured them. "I've never been better."

Indeed, her eyes were sparkling as she looked at the two of them and continued. "I heard your proposal to Elise, Derrick—and her acceptance." She put a hand over her chest and sighed. "My prayers have been answered."

Derrick sighed with relief, and he chuckled. "So have mine, Mama."

"And mine," Elise added as Derrick pulled her into the circle of his arms once more.

"I am so thankful," Derrick's mother said. "I don't know how much longer I could have pretended to feel bad, when all I've really been doing is trying to stir up a little romance between the two of you!"

"You haven't been sick?"

"Well, not lately. Since I got over the pneumonia, I've been fine." She grinned at them.

"Mama!" Derrick said. "We've been worried about you."

"Well, I could see the Lord at work, but you two just didn't always open your eyes to what He was showing you. I don't think He minded a little help from me. You both seemed to need all the help you could get! And I figured the more time you spent together, the better."

"Mama!" Elise shook her head and began to giggle.

"It worked, didn't it?"

Derrick looked into Elise's eyes and smiled. "It worked. Thank you, Mama."

He hugged Elise to him and sent up a prayer of thanksgiving. For he knew full well that it was the Lord who'd given him the best Christmas present ever. It certainly didn't bother Derrick that He might have used his mother to help things along.

⁊

Light snowflakes were indeed falling the next morning when Derrick went down to light the range so the kitchen would be warm for Elise and his mother. It was more than a little cold when he made his way over to the barn to do his chores and even colder on the way back. He was struck with a sudden idea, and he hurried back inside the house to see what Elise and his mother thought of it.

His bride-to-be was at the stove, an apron covering her Sunday dress. The look in her eyes and the smile she gave him told Derrick all he needed to know—last night was real and Elise did love him. He strode over to her and gathered her in his arms. "Good morning, my love," he whispered before lowering his lips to hers.

The sound of his mother clearing her throat broke them apart. But when he turned to look at her, Derrick could see she wasn't the least bit disturbed to find them kissing in the kitchen. She was grinning from ear to ear.

He smiled and winked at her. "I have an idea."

"Oh? What is it, son?"

"Well, I've waited so very long to have family with me at Christmastime. Do you think it would be all right if we open some presents today—before church?" He turned to Elise. "I've already got what I wanted for Christmas—Elise has promised to be my wife. But, Elise, I'd like for you and Mama to open what I got each of you. Please."

Elise grinned and glanced at his mother. She nodded. "It's all right with me, Mama, if it's all right with you."

"Please, Mama," Derrick implored his mother with a smile. She knew what he'd gotten for Elise, and he hoped she remembered and realized she could use it today.

"Well, if you think we have time." She looked at the clock on the wall. "It appears that we do. Evidently we were all so excited about you two finally admitting your love for one another that we didn't sleep as long as usual."

"I don't think I slept much at all last night," Derrick said, glancing over at Elise. "I couldn't wait for morning so I could see Elise again and make sure it wasn't all a dream."

"I felt the same way," Elise admitted, her cheeks coloring as she returned his smile.

"Well, obviously it was no dream. Or else we were all dreaming the same one," Frieda said with a chuckle. "Let's get breakfast over with, and then we can start unwrapping those presents."

&

They didn't linger over a second cup of coffee that morning. Instead, while Elise and Frieda cleared the table and did dishes, Derrick headed back out to the barn. Elise knew he was going to get his mother's present, and she could barely contain her excitement at the anticipation of seeing Frieda's reaction when she opened it. She had to giggle at the look on her mother-in-law's face when Derrick brought the crate inside and set it near the tree.

"This is yours, Mama."

"Oh, Derrick, that's very big. I can't imagine what you have in there," Frieda said as she dried her hands and hung the dish towel on a hook.

"Well, don't try. Just come open it."

Elise took off her apron and hurried to watch.

Derrick loosened the top of the crate and stood back as his mother opened her gift. "Oh! Oh, Derrick—a sewing machine!" she exclaimed. "You couldn't have gotten me anything I wanted more—well, besides you and Elise getting together!" She turned and gave Derrick a hug. "Oh, son, thank you!"

Tears gathered in Elise's eyes as she watched Frieda and Derrick. This was the most wonderful Christmas she'd ever had! The man she loved had asked her to marry him, and his mother would still be part of her family. Who could ask for more?

Derrick reached under the tree and handed her a large present. "For my bride-to-be."

Elise's heart felt near bursting with happiness. "You've already given me the present I wished for most, too. I don't need anything else."

"Oh, this you'll be able to use. Please, open it," Derrick said with a grin.

Elise had shaken the package a few times when she'd been in the kitchen with no one else around, but she still didn't have any idea what it was. She laid the box on the kitchen table and carefully unwrapped it. She took the top off the box and caught her breath. Inside was the beautiful wool cloak she'd seen when they were out shopping. She hadn't been aware that Derrick had even noticed her looking at it. "Oh, Derrick," she breathed as she lifted the cloak out of the box and held it up for Frieda to see. "It's lovely—and just the right weight for this winter weather."

"I thought it might come in handy today. It's getting quite cold out," Derrick said.

Elise rushed to hug his neck. "You are so very thoughtful. Thank you so much. I can't wait to wear it." She turned back to the tree, picked up a small package, and handed it to Derrick. "Now it's your turn."

He quickly tore the paper off and smiled at what he saw. "*In His Steps*! Oh, thank you, Elise. I really wanted this book—I've heard it's excellent." He pulled her close and gave her a hug. "I'll treasure it always because it came from you." He reluctantly released her and said, "But that's all we have time for now."

"Are you sure? You've waited a long time—"

Derrick pulled her to his side and shook his head. "No, we really don't have time. We'll wait until tomorrow for the rest. I just wanted you to have the cloak to wear to church today. . . and for Mama to have her sewing machine."

"But—"

Derrick ended her objection by placing a gentle kiss on her lips. He broke it off and looked deep into her eyes. "There's no other present I need—but to settle a date for our wedding. If we get there a little early, maybe we can talk to Harold before services."

Elise wasn't about to argue with that. She couldn't wait to be able to call this wonderful man her husband. She slipped on the first Christmas gift he'd given her, knowing she would cherish it each time she wore it in the coming years. "I'm ready whenever you two are."

❧

Snowflakes were still falling gently as they made their way to church on Christmas Eve, promising a white Christmas for the next day. Derrick and Elise were anxious to talk to Harold and see when he could preside over a wedding, hoping it could be during the next week. But before they had a chance, his mother took charge, pulling the preacher to the side as soon as they got to church. After several nods and grins, Harold came over to them.

"You know, I wanted to thank you for giving me the opportunity to be part of the happiness you made possible for the Hanson and Ballard families. It truly was a joy to see their expressions when I gave them your gifts. And the basket you gave Rachel and me. . . Thank you for your thoughtfulness. Your mother says there might be something I can do for you in return. How would you like to be married today, right after services?"

"Oh, well, yes, of course I'd like to," Derrick said, "but I don't have a ring for Elise yet, and—"

His mother pulled the simple band his father had given her off her finger and handed it to him. "You can use this until you can get her one, son."

"But, Mama, Elise might not—"

Elise rushed to assure him. It was all he wanted for Christmas, after all. "It's fine, Derrick. I don't need a ring to prove we're married. All we need are witnesses and a preacher to marry us. We certainly have that today."

"You're sure? I'll buy you a ring right after Christmas."

Her heart was filled with so much love, Elise felt it might burst. "I'm sure."

"Then yes, Harold," her husband-to-be said, "we'd love to have you to marry us after services today."

"Consider it done."

At first Elise was afraid she wouldn't be able to keep her mind on the sermon Harold brought to them as she sat beside Derrick. But as soon as the preacher began speaking, he had her full attention, for he brought a lovely lesson on God's love to them, reminding them that He brought His only Son to this earth that all might have the hope of salvation through Him. What greater love could there be than that?

That the Lord loved her had never been clearer to Elise than today. He'd provided for her salvation through His precious Son, but He'd also provided for her happiness here on this earth. He'd answered all of her prayers. And He'd answered abundantly.

Oh, she was going back to Denver, but it would be as Derrick's wife and only to pack up her belongings and put her house up for sale. It would be their wedding trip after the first of the year. And her beloved mother-in-law would still be just that. The Lord had shown her over and over again just how much He loved her.

Elise felt surrounded by His love now, as the service ended and Harold asked everyone to remain seated for their wedding. The congregation seemed quite happy to stay a little longer for the simple ceremony.

As Elise stood beside Derrick and they said their vows, she felt overwhelmed by the joy she felt. When Derrick kissed her for the first time as his wife, Elise returned his kiss with a heart full of love.

"I present to you Mr. and Mrs. Derrick Morgan," Harold said as they turned to face the congregation.

They walked down the aisle as husband and wife, and Elise sent up a silent prayer, thanking the Lord above for answering all of her prayers and for giving her a new love, a new home, and a new life. She would be forever grateful.

A Letter To Our Readers

Dear Reader:
In order that we might better contribute to your reading enjoyment, we would appreciate your taking a few minutes to respond to the following questions. We welcome your comments and read each form and letter we receive. When completed, please return to the following:

Fiction Editor
Heartsong Presents
PO Box 719
Uhrichsville, Ohio 44683

1. Did you enjoy reading *Stirring Up Romance* by Janet Lee Barton?
   ❏ Very much! I would like to see more books by this author!
   ❏ Moderately. I would have enjoyed it more if

   _____

   _____

   _____

2. Are you a member of **Heartsong Presents**? ❏ Yes ❏ No
   If no, where did you purchase this book? _____

   _____

3. How would you rate, on a scale from 1 (poor) to 5 (superior), the cover design? _____

4. On a scale from 1 (poor) to 10 (superior), please rate the following elements.

   ____ Heroine   ____ Plot
   ____ Hero   ____ Inspirational theme
   ____ Setting   ____ Secondary characters

5. These characters were special because? _____
   _____
   _____

6. How has this book inspired your life? _____
   _____
   _____

7. What settings would you like to see covered in future
   Heartsong Presents books? _____
   _____
   _____

8. What are some inspirational themes you would like to see
   treated in future books? _____
   _____
   _____

9. Would you be interested in reading other **Heartsong
   Presents** titles? ❏ Yes ❏ No

10. Please check your age range:
    ❏ Under 18   ❏ 18-24
    ❏ 25-34   ❏ 35-45
    ❏ 46-55   ❏ Over 55

Name _____
Occupation _____
Address _____
City, State, Zip_____